FIVE GREEN MEN

Nancy's vacation at her aunt's San Francisco mansion takes a nightmarish turn when she is attacked by a mysterious thief of ancient jade figurines. Her assailant's vows to kill her are very nearly successful more than once. Can she trust the stranger who has been following her ever since her arrival in the city, even though his intervention saves her life? Then she must contend with a murder she is powerless to stop, and the return of her father, who she'd been told had died when she was a child . . .

V. J. BANIS

FIVE GREEN MEN

Complete and Unabridged

LINFORD
Leicester

First published in Great Britain

First Linford Edition
published 2015

A catalogue record for this book is available
from the British Library.

ISBN 978–1–4448–2482–7

Published by
F. A. Thorpe (Publishing)
Anstey, Leicestershire

Set by Words & Graphics Ltd.
Anstey, Leicestershire
Printed and bound in Great Britain by
T. J. International Ltd., Padstow, Cornwall

This book is printed on acid-free paper

1

Nancy Dunbar came up the steep hill from the cable car stop, leaning forward. It was nearly noon and the morning fog had begun to lift. A foghorn called from the harbor; wind chimes tinkled in a doorway. A squealing violin from one of the apartments she passed seemed to mock her:

'Jilted lover,' it called. 'Jilted lover.'

At the corner she glanced back the way she had come and saw a man in a white jacket. She had seen him on the cable car as well. She hadn't seen him get off the car when she did but there he was, very determinedly studying the merchandise in a shop window. *It is probably only coincidence,* she thought, crossing the street. Just a week before, however, another stewardess who worked for the same airlines as she did had been accosted in broad daylight on a downtown Chicago street.

When she looked again, however, the man wasn't in sight. 'Men have a way of disappearing out of my life,' she said to herself sardonically. Since that last scene with Ken, she had been flailing herself with her unworthiness.

Her aunt Polly's house was often called a mansion in those books on historical San Francisco houses. In fact it was small, with a narrow front that looked bigger than it was. Nancy let herself in the front door with the key her aunt had given her years ago. This was Tuesday. Ellen, the maid, was off Tuesdays and it was her aunt's day for the hairdresser.

She wasn't exactly expected. Her vacation had been scheduled to begin next week and she had dropped her aunt a note saying she might spend a few days with her, but yesterday her supervisor had looked at her with a critical eye. 'Look, honey,' she said, 'it's none of my business, except the way you look, you're liable to scare the passengers. Why don't you start your vacation early?'

There hadn't been time to tell her aunt of the change, but that really was not necessary. In theory at least she had lived with her aunt as a young girl, although in fact she had spent most of her time at boarding schools and summer camps. She and Aunt Polly had rarely spent more than a week or so together at any one time. Still, however tenuous the relationship, she had looked upon this house as 'home', and although she now shared an apartment with two other stewardesses in Los Angeles, she had no qualms about appearing here earlier than announced.

'Anybody home?' she called, only as a matter of form. She took off her coat and scarf, leaving them on the coat tree in the hall and went through the arch into the parlor. The creaking of a floorboard made her turn, and she saw the man.

She realized at once that he must have been behind the door, pressed against the wall, when she came in and was trying now to steal away, but he turned as she did, realizing that the creaking floorboard had heralded his presence.

She had been exposed to physical danger only rarely and the sensation of fear was unfamiliar to her. She drew in her breath sharply.

For a moment neither of them moved.

She had a sense of unreality. In the distance she heard the clanging of a cable car climbing the hill. The intruder had long, thick hair and a heavy beard, and his eyes were hidden behind dark sunglasses. He wore jeans with colorful patches sewn on them. He might have been any of the thousands of bearded men in this city.

The fear broke finally. She whirled and ran toward the phone. She reached it and was even able to dial the operator, but the line was still buzzing when he grabbed the instrument from her hand and pulled the wire free from the wall.

She tried to scream, but his arm went about her throat, crushing her with his strength. She saw his nicotine-stained fingers, and a scar on the back of his hand.

She clawed his arm but she was strangling, losing her strength. Her knees buckled and the room careened violently.

She kicked at his shin. For a second or two, his grip loosened and she had a taste of air, but it was not enough. His arm tightened. Darkness closed in upon her.

★   ★   ★

On the street outside, the man in the white jacket lit another cigarette and wondered if there were any significance to the niece's unexpected arrival. It might be just coincidence. On the other hand, he had been trained to look upon anything unexpected as significant. Until now, he had checked out the niece only as a matter of routine, a relative who lived in Los Angeles. Now she was here, in San Francisco. She would merit closer watching.

He had turned to go when a bearded man in patched jeans came out of the door he had been watching and moved swiftly up the street.

The man in the white jacket began to run. It might only be another coincidence; this might not be the same bearded man he had been looking for. But, coincidence on top of coincidence?

He reached the corner. For a moment it seemed as if the bearded man had vanished into thin air.

A car's engine coughed to life and a

Volkswagen parked down the street shot away from the curb, darting in front of an oncoming car, and causing a squeal of brakes. In another minute, the Volkswagen was gone from sight.

* * *

'Hysteria,' Polly Dunbar was fond of saying, 'is unbecoming in any woman. In a woman of my years it is disgusting.' To Polly Dunbar's way of thinking, virtually any display of emotion came under the heading of hysteria. She reacted to sentimental scenes and distressing circumstances for the most part with the same slightly reproving smile.

It was in much the same way that she reacted to the scene she found when she arrived home. Nothing ever shattered the icy poise for which she was known.

She came up the steps as she always did, slowly. She fancied that people were watching her enter this elegant home and she moved slowly to savor their envy. She never looked to see if anyone was in fact watching, and if her eye happened to fall

6

upon someone, they were not likely to be warmed by the look. Her lips were habitually compressed and she had a way of looking at people as if she thought them a bit stupid. She had never gotten from a human being the feeling of deeply abiding pleasure that she got from inserting her key in the lock of this fine old Victorian mansion.

She shed her coat and hat and gloves and came into the parlor, pausing just inside the door. One eyebrow lifted in surprise, but she gave no cry of alarm. Her multi-ringed hand did not fly to her mouth.

Her cynical eyes took in the scene quickly and settled finally upon her niece sprawled somewhat inelegantly upon the floor. For a fraction of a second they went to the green men across the room, and back to her niece.

She stooped down to feel for a pulse and finding it, she listened for a moment, then rose and went to the kitchen for a wet towel.

★   ★   ★

7

Nancy woke in the bedroom that was hers whenever she stayed at her aunt's house. Her head ached and her throat was sore. She had just awakened when her aunt came in and regarded her critically.

'You came early,' she said. 'I wasn't expecting you until next week.'

'I took an extra week. I . . . there was a man here when I came in. He knocked me unconscious.'

'I suspected something had happened,' Polly said drily.

'Did he . . . was anything taken?'

'Nothing. I presume you interrupted him too soon. Can you sit up?'

'I think so.' She sat up with her aunt's help. 'How did I get here?'

'I called Doctor Williams and he helped me get you to bed. He also left a sedative for you. Here, drink this.'

'I must say, you don't seem particularly upset by a burglary.'

'An *attempted* burglary. Of course, I'm annoyed. However, I have just suffered nearly two hours of discomfort and paid a scandalous charge to have my hair twisted into its present unnatural state, and I have

8

no intention of pulling it out now. Lie down.'

Nancy sank gratefully into the softness of the pillows, willing enough for the moment to allow her aunt to take charge. After a moment, her eyes fluttered open. 'The police. Have you called the police yet?'

'I'll attend to that.' Already her aunt's voice sounded far away. The sedative was strong, and fast-acting. Nancy felt herself gently floating into a soothing darkness.

'What do you suppose he was after?' she asked sleepily.

'Why, the green men, of course.'

Of course, Nancy thought. Of all the gems in this gem of a house, surely the green men were the most outstanding. But that man with the beard hadn't gotten them.

She almost thought she could feel his fingers again upon her throat, squeezing, squeezing.

She slept.

★ ★ ★

When she awoke, the room was dark and she experienced a brief, recurring fear of darkness. Something had happened when she was little, something connected with the dark and her room, but she could not remember what. It was before she had come to live with Aunt Polly, and she often thought that it was somehow associated with her father, but that may have been merely fantasy on her part.

Her father was the object of many fantasies. She remembered nothing factual about him. He had disappeared when she had been very young. Later, when she had been old enough to notice the absence in their lives, she had asked her mother why she did not have a father like the other children in their Chicago neighborhood.

'Your father has gone away for a while,' her mother invariably explained.

'Will he come back?'

Her mother had looked a little sad, and for a long time she said nothing. Eventually she said only, 'Perhaps.'

A photograph of a man sat atop her mother's dresser. Gradually Nancy had come to realize that this was a photograph of her father. He was a handsome, strong-looking man, with laughing eyes that seemed to meet hers when she looked at the picture.

Nancy's memories of those early years were dim — she had been no more than four or so at the time. She remembered that they were very poor, and her mother had taken in sewing; but even so, some evenings dinner was not quite adequate to still the pangs of hunger.

One incident stuck in her mind. A letter came one day. Her mother read it and began to cry. Nancy had never seen her mother cry before, and it frightened her so that she too began to cry, without knowing why. Her mother had comforted her and told her there was nothing to cry about. She put her to bed; but Nancy, unable to sleep, got out of bed and went to her mother's room.

There she had seen her mother crying again, holding the picture of Nancy's father as if talking to it. While Nancy watched, she kissed the cold lips of the photograph. A great sob escaped her throat and she threw herself across the bed.

Nancy crept back to her own bed and, still without understanding, cried herself to sleep. After that, whenever she was upset, she followed her mother's example and took her troubles to the man in the photograph.

She learned afterward that her mother's father, her grandfather, had died, and this was the news the letter had brought. Nancy was left in the care of a neighbor woman and Nancy's mother went away for a week, to San Francisco, to attend the funeral. Nancy had never before heard of any relatives, except her missing father, and she could not help but wonder what other relatives she had in that distant city.

'You have an aunt,' her mother admitted when pressed. 'Aunt Polly.'

'Will I ever meet her?'

'Someday, perhaps.'

Nancy met her Aunt Polly sooner than expected. After that trip to San Francisco, her mother had seemed increasingly dispirited. Less than a year later, she came down with a cold that became pneumonia. Nancy went again to stay with the neighbor woman.

She never saw her mother again. A few days later, a strange woman came for her.

This was her aunt Polly, and she explained in a business-like fashion that Nancy was coming to San Francisco to live with her. She did not sound particularly happy about this fact; even to Nancy's young ears she sounded more resigned than anything. She was much older than Nancy's mother had been, and to a child she seemed ancient.

If she was neither loving nor warm, however, neither was she cruel or selfish. Nancy, who had often lacked enough to eat and clothes enough to dress properly for school, found that she was now, through her aunt, quite wealthy. She was at once given a luxurious room of her own. She no longer rode buses, except occasionally for fun as she got older. Now limousines and taxis took her wherever she had to go. She had a splendid new wardrobe; and instead of a public school, she was whisked off to a very exclusive girls' school.

At first Nancy had suffered from the lack of affection she received from her aunt, thinking that she was unlovable. She had tried to take this problem to the photograph of her father, which she had brought with her to San Francisco, but now the laughing eyes seemed to mock her. Hadn't he, too, gone away? Hadn't he, too, found her lacking?

The photograph was one of the few things over which she and her aunt ever clashed. For the most part, Aunt Polly was soft but firm-spoken, and she allowed her niece a great deal of independence within the framework of a life organized to keep them apart as much as possible. One day, however, she had come into Nancy's room and found her niece talking to the photograph of her father. Something about the scene infuriated her and she snatched the photo away.

'It's unhealthy for you to go on like this with a picture,' she said. 'Your father is dead.'

Nancy cried and begged to be allowed to keep the photograph, but her aunt sternly refused and took it away. Nancy never saw it again.

In time she came to see that her aunt's nature was simply not an affectionate one. Polly Dunbar's affections were for things, not people: things she could collect and own, for which other people could envy her. Her belongings were not merely belongings; they were her lovers and friends. She was a woman, as one society figure had put it, who was often invited, but never welcomed.

When she was old enough to reason these things out for herself, Nancy lost the resentment that she had come to feel toward her aunt. Understanding made her, in fact, feel rather vaguely affectionate toward her aunt, who had at the very least taken her in without any hesitation and provided most generously for her in every material way. Her feeling that she was somehow inadequate, however, lingered. She never quite outgrew the idea that she was unlovable.

Ken had confirmed that, hadn't he? He had joined West Coast Airlines six months before as a pilot, and from their first meeting, it looked as if this was to be the romance of the decade. And for a few months, it had been. Then, with a snap of the fingers, he had declared that it was over; that he 'didn't want things to get complicated.'

She could look at the whole thing logically, of course, and see that the breakup was inevitable. She had known from the start that Ken was a spoiled child. Maybe that had even been part of his appeal. Anyone could tell he was far from being ready to settle down with one woman. So, his rejection of her now had no real significance. But that didn't stop it from triggering the old, self-blaming reactions. It was all well and good to understand their roots and to say that she could be loved just like any other woman, but the simple truth was, nobody did love her.

She made a grimace, angry with herself for these self-pitying thoughts, and sat up in bed, flicking on the light.

The telephone beside the bed rang. 'Nancy?' a deep masculine voice asked when she answered it.

'Yes?' She did not recognize the voice, but the airlines sometimes called.

'Get out of town, for your own safety.'

'What . . . who is this?' There was no reply and after a moment, she realized that the caller had hung up.

2

For Polly Dunbar, it was an imposition to have her niece in the house just now. She had done what she considered her duty by the girl. She had promised her sister that she would take care of the child, and she had done so to the best of her capabilities. She could not give what she did not have to give. In her own way, she was fond of her niece, however; perhaps the more so because Nancy had proven herself of an independent spirit too, so that she was not much of a hindrance.

At first, Polly had lived in terror that a small child in the house might stain the upholstery or break the china or run screaming up and down stairs. Fortunately a combination of good manners and a withdrawn nature in her niece spared her these catastrophes. With Nancy largely occupied at schools and summer camps, they were able to get accustomed to one another

17

very gradually, over a long period of time, so that now she had no fears that Nancy would tie her down or impede her life-style.

Now, unexpectedly, her niece's visit had altered certain circumstances. She sat in the living room thinking of these things and ignored the ringing of the telephone, noting half-consciously that Nancy had answered it upstairs. After several minutes, she heard Nancy descending the stairs. Polly looked at her critically.

'You look terrible,' she said simply. It was not meant to be unkind, but merely a statement of fact. Nancy looked nearly as white as the robe she had slipped into. The bruises were shockingly visible at her throat, and her face wore a drawn, hunted look.

'Someone just called,' Nancy said in a small, dry voice. 'He told me to leave town.'

'Who was it? And why did he say you should leave town?'

'I don't know who it was. He didn't say. He just said to leave town — that it was for my own safety.'

'Some crank, I imagine,' Polly said, unperturbed. 'There's a lot of that sort of thing these days.'

'But he knew my name.'

'It wouldn't have been some jilted boyfriend, would it?' Polly fixed her stern gaze on her. 'There was a case just a few weeks ago, where a jilted boyfriend broke into the house and tried to murder the entire family.'

'No, there's no one.' Nancy paused. 'He wouldn't have called. Anyway, I know his voice. And I didn't jilt him . . . ' She stopped, embarrassed. 'I guess you're right, it was just some crank. But it's unnerving. Did you call the police about that other business?'

'That's all been taken care of. Would you like a cup of coffee? There's some in the kitchen.'

'I could use some, thanks.'

'Would you come back here with it? There's something I want to talk about.'

The coffee was in an electric percolator. Brewing coffee electrically was pretty much the extent of her aunt's culinary skills. Nancy poured a cup, adding plenty

19

of sugar, and brought it with her back to the living room.

As she sat in the chair facing Polly, Nancy's eyes fell upon the curio cabinet, glass-doored and lighted softly from within. The cabinet held only three objects — three jade figures of old men, obviously Chinese, done in a pale jade the green of the crest of an ocean wave, lighted from behind by the afternoon sun. The delicate carving of the figures had blurred slightly through the centuries since the carver had first fashioned them with gentle hands. They were very old and literally priceless, the chief source of her aunt's pride-of-possession.

'Thank Heaven that man didn't get them,' Nancy said aloud. 'You really ought to have them put away somewhere safe, you know.'

'Where I could never see them? Thank you, no.'

Nancy smiled. It was so like Aunt Polly to cherish things above people, but refuse to take the steps to insure their safety. Nancy had finally relaxed a little after the phone call. She could be grateful for one thing, though: this was the first time in weeks she had not been thinking of Ken and that stupid break-up.

She took a sip of the hot coffee. 'You said you wanted to talk about something?'

Polly was never one to beat around the bush, and having decided that this subject had to be broached, she did so now in a brutally frank manner. 'Yes, it's about your father. He's in San Francisco.'

'My father?' The coffee cup slipped from Nancy's hand, scattering broken china and coffee across the floor.

Polly gave a cry of distress and leaped to her feet. 'The rug!' she cried.

'But, Aunt Polly . . . ?'

'We've got to clean that up before it stains.' Polly disappeared into the kitchen.

Nancy was only barely aware of her aunt scolding and clucking as she cleaned up the spilled coffee and the broken cup. Her thoughts were spinning through her head. Her father was dead, wasn't he? What could Aunt Polly have meant? But if he wasn't dead . . . ? The man in the photograph, the one she had always longed for?

At last Polly returned to the sofa, having repaired the damage to the rug. 'Well,' she said, 'after that dramatic interruption . . . My dear, you are entitled to your emotional reactions, of course, but not at the expense of my carpet, please.'

'Aunt Polly, please, tell me, what did you mean when you said my father was here in San Francisco?'

'Just that,' Polly said in a matter-of-fact voice.

'But — but he's dead. You told me that yourself, years ago.'

'It wasn't true. Not then, nor now. I wanted you to think he was dead. I thought that as far as we were concerned, he was dead. I was mistaken. He is here, in San Francisco, and he wants to see you. Frankly, I meant to see him tomorrow and order him to leave the city. But now you've shown up sooner than I expected. It seemed inevitable that the two of you would meet and I thought it best that I prepare you for the event beforehand.'

Nancy managed a wan smile and a

glance at the carpet. 'It could hardly be more of a shock.'

'Yes, well, that wasn't exactly what I meant. I thought you ought to be told about him, so that you would know the truth before he tried to give you any cock-and-bull stories. He will, undoubtedly.'

Nancy started to say something and then caught herself. 'Perhaps you should tell me the whole story,' she said instead. Although she was fairly boiling over with excitement, she forced herself to assume an air of relaxation. Her training as a stewardess helped her to look unconcerned.

'Yes.' Polly paused for a moment, considering how to begin. 'Your father, Harvey Blair, was from here originally, as of course was your mother, my sister, Elizabeth. Your real name is Nancy Blair, not Dunbar, but I had reasons for insisting that you use the name Dunbar, which I think you'll appreciate when you've heard everything.

'Harvey Blair was a scoundrel in every way. Your grandfather, my father, warned Elizabeth about the man, but she wouldn't listen. They married and when Grandfather ordered your mother from the house and disinherited her, the newlyweds went to Chicago. Frankly, I agreed entirely with my father. The man was worthless and Elizabeth was doubly a fool not only to marry him, but to go far away with him, to Chicago.'

'But if they loved one another . . . '

Polly gave a disdainful snort. 'Loved one another? She loved him — in a stupid fashion, of course. As for him, he married her because of the money. If he had thought he could twist me about his finger the way he did her, he'd have married me, or tried to at least.'

Something in Aunt Polly's tone flashed a light in Nancy's mind. A note of — what? Jealousy? Had Polly Dunbar been in love with the same man, who had thrown her over for the pretty younger sister?

'But that doesn't explain why he went away. Or why I was told he was dead.'

'I wanted to spare you the shame of knowing that as well as being a scoundrel, he was a thief.'

'How can you say that?'

'Because it's true. Your father committed robbery. He robbed a bank.'

'That can't be true. Surely there was some mistake.'

'There was no mistake. After his arrest, he confessed. It was not his only crime. He and his partners had been involved in several robberies. They went to prison. He's been in prison until just a few weeks ago.'

Nancy sank back into her chair, overcome with a sense of shame and grief. The man she had idolized all these years, the man to whose picture her mother — and she herself — had wept and prayed . . . a common criminal.

'The shame of it hastened my father's death, in my opinion,' Polly went on, speaking harshly. 'Fortunately, this was all in Chicago. The marriage had never been publicized here, so the names weren't linked by the press and almost no one realized there was a connection. Because of his confession, the trial was brief, so there was little publicity. Your father went to prison. Soon after, your mother took ill and died. I went to Chicago and brought you here. I wrote your father and told him I would see that you were brought up properly, but in return he must never try to see you, or ever let anyone know that you were his daughter. I told him I had told you he was dead, and it must remain so.'

Nancy sat in stunned silence. Her initial reaction had been one of shock and even of resentment against her father. Still, the childish longing persisted. She wanted to see him; yes, and wanted to forgive him, if he would ask forgiveness. What he had done did not alter the fact that he was her father.

As she had time to weigh her aunt's story, she found too that there was a great deal to be read between the lines. Her father and mother had defied disinheritance and disapproval to marry and had gone to Chicago. That indicated that they had been truly in love and that her father had not married for any hoped-for wealth.

At least, it could be interpreted that way. She did not know what his motives had been for committing robbery, but he had confessed and paid his debt to society. In the interim he had lost his wife and given up his daughter so that she could be raised in comfort and without scandal. This was the act of a generous and loving man; surely during those years he must have longed for his daughter, just as she had longed for him. Moreover, his pain must have been worse, because he knew that she was alive somewhere, separated from him.

She had been haunted since childhood by the belief that her father had not loved her and had gone away. Now it seemed that he might, after all, have loved her very deeply; and for that, she was willing to forgive him a great deal.

Aunt Polly, breaking the lengthy silence, said, 'Now, as I might have known he would, he's broken his word. He wants to see you. Frankly, I expected you up in a week and by then I would have dealt with him. But, here you are. And I suppose you will want to meet him for yourself.'

'Yes I do, very much.'

Polly looked at her shrewdly. 'You

won't find any regal figure out of your childish dreams, my dear. Whatever picture you've carried of him in your mind, you will be disappointed by the reality. One always is.'

'Whatever faulty stuff he's made of, he's my father. I want to meet him.'

'And so you shall,' Aunt Polly said decisively.

★   ★   ★

Nancy spoke briefly to her father that same evening on the telephone. There was not, as she might have imagined, a flash of recognition at the sound of his voice. It was the voice of a stranger, weak and rasping, so that it did not even call up the face of that laughing, determined man in the old photograph.

They made arrangements to meet the following day. For some reason he did not want her to come to where he was staying, and they deliberated over one or two public places.

Finally he said, 'Down at the waterfront there's an old sailing ship that's been

28

made into a sort of museum. Do you know it?'

'Yes, the *Balclutha*. I'll meet you there, shall we say about ten in the morning?'

'Yes.' There was a pause. 'How will I know you?'

She winced, thinking what a horrible question that was between a father and daughter. 'I'll wear a yellow cloth coat,' she said.

She slept poorly that night. She thought of her father and wondered if that mysterious call she had gotten had anything to do with him and his sudden reappearance in her life.

She was ready quite early in the morning. She had wakened for the last time just after dawn and admitted to herself the impossibility of getting back to sleep. She took her time dressing, choosing a navy blue shirtwaist because it would make the yellow coat stand out all the more, and added a navy scarf.

Aunt Polly, who ordinarily slept late, was at the breakfast table when she came down. Nancy had just taken a seat when Ellen, her aunt's housekeeper and maid, came in from the kitchen bearing a dish of fresh warm rolls.

'Good morning Miss Nancy,' she said with a grin as warm as the rolls. 'I see you've come sooner than expected. It's good to have you back.'

'Thank you. It's good to be here.'

Ellen had been with Aunt Polly as long as Nancy could remember, and whatever affection the little-girl-Nancy had gotten in this house had come from Ellen, who had taken her for walks or to the zoo or the park; and it was Ellen to whom she had come crying whenever she scuffed a knee or cut a finger. Ellen had tucked her into bed at night and sometimes stayed with her to help her overcome her fear of the dark.

Polly surveyed her niece coolly, her eyes lingering on the topaz ring on Nancy's finger. 'Is it wise to wear that?' she asked, buttering a roll.

'You surely don't think he's going to try to steal my ring?'

'He's been in prison for stealing. I've wondered why he should feel it so important to come here now and it has occurred to me that he knows I'm wealthy and might assume that you share that wealth to some extent.'

'He might also have come because his wife died while he was in prison, and I am his daughter, and all that is left of that part of his life.'

Polly raised her eyes only briefly from her roll. 'Perhaps,' she said.

3

It was a crisp, clear morning. Nancy walked to the cable car line, enjoying the city. Although technically it had been her home since she was a child, she had rarely spent more than a few days at a time here, so that its charm had never dulled for her.

Every city, of course, had its own personality, but one was more aware of San Francisco's. In Los Angeles people rushed about in cars, and in New York they rushed about underground, but in San Francisco they rode the cable cars, or they walked — at a leisurely pace because of the steep hills. San Francisco was a street city, a city of flower vendors and self-conscious quaintness, a true melting pot of languages and cultures and life styles. On the cable cars a grande dame in mink rode beside a bearded and barefoot hippie, neither seeming to mind the other.

Most of all, everywhere was the air

— that glorious breeze from the sea, redolent of the ocean smells, crisp, sometimes freezing, always invigorating. It seemed to sweep away the cobwebs of gloom that one had accumulated elsewhere, flinging them away with a cheery hand like trivial feathers.

She got off the cable car at the end of line, a few blocks from Fisherman's Wharf. It was not much after ten but already the streets were crowded. What a polyglot mass of people they were — tourists in plaid shorts with cameras about their necks, shivering because no one had warned them that the city is cool even in late summer; a Japanese girl in a kimono, looking as if she had just stepped from a picture book, *Tales of Old Japan*; a group of sailors from some foreign navy, drifting along in a tightly knit group that belied the bravado they tried to assume; a group of hippie street musicians warming up; street vendors selling fresh shrimp and crab from steaming wagons. The smell of fish was omnipresent, as were the roar of a thousand voices and the lapping of the water on the piles just to her left.

By the time she approached the *Balclutha*, the old cargo ship made into a floating museum, she had almost forgotten her previous mood of gloom and worry. At the sight of the ramp leading to the deck above she had a moment of panic, an impulse to turn and leave without keeping her rendezvous. Perhaps it was better to let the dead bury the dead.

She told herself firmly, *He isn't dead; he never was.* Only, she had been allowed to think so. She paid the entry fee and walked quickly up the ramp, her heels making little clicking sounds.

She was not the first aboard. A middle-aged man stood at the stern and looked longingly across the waters. He started guiltily as a small boy ran up to tell him about something below and the two of them disappeared down a wooden stair.

It was still early. Nancy strolled along the deck, contrasting the ship with the sleek jets she travelled in almost every day. The galley, or kitchen, was a small structure by itself on the main deck. It was open now at both sides, so that one could see through it. She wondered what manner of man could have turned out a decent meal in this pathetic cubbyhole. Worse, having prepared the dinner for his captain, the cook had had to emerge onto this deck, sometimes in a violent storm, and make his way along the pitching deck to the captain's quarters. She wondered how many meals, and their cooks with them, went into the sea.

She might not have enjoyed the role of cook on one of these sea ships, but certainly she could have settled comfortably into the elegant rooms furnished for the skipper. All that polished wood and gleaming brass. An organ stood in one corner, and a shelf with books held in place by a brass gallery.

She glanced at her watch. It was near eleven. She went out onto the deck and took a place by the rail from where she could see anyone boarding the ship and they could see her.

She almost did not place him at first, because she had been expecting one man, not two. She did notice them, however, because they seemed so . . . furtive was not quite the right word. Hesitant perhaps was better. They went slowly past the ship's entrance, glancing at it and up the ramp, and turning around came back. It looked like they couldn't make up their minds whether to board the ship or not.

They did not seem to notice her. They looked up and down the street and at the ship. One of them was much younger. The older of the two might have been sixty or seventy, but the other, as nearly as Nancy could judge, was no more than thirty or thirty-five.

The younger one, with another timid glance around, said something. The older glanced up and looked at her, although his eyes slid away almost at once. He seemed to reach a decision and purchased tickets for both of them. They did not look up again, but kept their eyes on the ground.

They came, though, straight to her. She stood, uncertain herself and frightened, waiting for them.

Not until he had reached where she waited did the older of the two men look up at her face. She saw then that she had been mistaken; that he was no more than perhaps fifty years old.

'You're Nancy?' he asked in a shy, small voice.

She nodded, mute for a moment before she managed to say, 'And you're — you're my father.'

How many times had she imagined this scene, from her childhood on? How many variations had there been in the playing of it? Never had she imagined a scene like this one, on the suddenly cold deck of a one-time sailing ship; this coming face-to-face with a stranger. She heard herself saying in a voice that was not her own, 'How do you do,' and she held her hand out stiffly.

He took it, muttering some greeting that she barely heard, and nodded his head toward the younger man. 'This is Mickey.'

An awful silence descended. After a moment she said, 'Have you had lunch? There's a restaurant over there where we can get something.'

'Some coffee, maybe,' her father said,

'and something sweet. Mick's got a sweet tooth, and where we were, there weren't many sweets.' He sounded embarrassed to say it, and at the same time defensive.

She would have liked to say, 'I understand,' but she didn't yet, and couldn't mouth anything so insincere, not at a time like this. She only nodded and managed a wan smile, and they went silently down the ramp to the street. She studied their reflections in the shop windows they passed. They both wore ill-cut suits that fit them poorly. She thought she remembered that men being discharged from prison were given a suit to wear.

Her father was of medium height and somewhat stocky. His face was colorless and deeply lined, and it was this that had made him seem so much older at first glance. Although he was obviously timid and still had that furtiveness about him, he had a certain air of determination also.

She wondered why the younger man had come along for what certainly should have been a private meeting. He was as sallow and colorless, but his skin was still smooth and unlined. He looked as if he had been ill; but that, she thought, was probably from his pasty complexion.

In a half hour or so the restaurant would be packed, but now they had no trouble getting a table by a window that overlooked the wharf. They asked for coffee, and her father ordered a piece of lemon pie for Mick, to the waiter's surprise.

'I brought Mick along because he doesn't like to be alone,' Harvey Blair said. 'Neither of us does. We've been together so long, we don't feel right if we're separated.'

'You were together in . . . ' She paused. ' . . . there?'

He nodded; the waiter came just then with the coffees and Mick's pie. He attacked it greedily, with only a glance at her and another, delighted, at her father.

'We got paroled the same time,' her father said. 'I could have gotten out six months sooner, but I didn't put in for parole until he was eligible too. I knew if I left, he'd just get into trouble.'

Mick had finished the pie in not much more than a minute. He wiped at his mouth and said, 'He took care of me the whole time I was in.'

She thought they felt a need to justify themselves and she did not know how to tell them it wasn't necessary. In a way she thought that the fatherly love she had longed for over so many years had been given instead to the man seated at her right. She might have resented it, but she could not help being glad that it had made things a bit easier for him.

'He was just a kid when he got there,' Harvey said. 'Lost among all those cut-throats. Someone had to look after him. There was one man, a convicted murderer, who kept bothering him. I had to straighten him out, and after that everyone left Mick alone.'

'What did you do?'

'I ripped his stomach open with a knife,' he said, as simply as a man might say, 'It's a nice day, isn't it?'

His eyes met hers boldly. For an instant she saw a ghost of the laughing eyes from the photograph — the first sense of familiarity she'd felt, though it was gone at once.

'In there, things are different. You learn

different values. It's hard to retain any sense of honor. I was lucky I had Mick. No matter how bad things would get, he could always think of something to make me laugh.' He turned to Mick, a grin lighting his face briefly. 'What was it you said that time about that guy got his throat cut in the dining room?'

Nancy's cup rattled on her saucer. Her father's smile faded.

'I don't remember now,' he finished lamely. 'It's gone clean out of my head. But at the time I couldn't stop laughing.'

Another awkward silence fell. After a long moment she asked, 'Would you like some money?'

'No, we have a little, thanks. You see, you work in there and they pay you wages for it. Not much, but if you hang on to it, it adds up over the years.'

Another silence. So much for Aunt Polly's theories.

'So you're my daughter.'

She was embarrassed, and only nodded. Mick was looking away, out the window.

'You don't remember me at all, do you?'

'No. There was a photograph of you. That's all I remember.'

'And your mother?'

'I remember her.'

He nodded, looking grim. *He remembers too,* she thought, and was suddenly moved by a wave of emotion from the past. He had loved, loved deeply, and had lost. A sense of grief — for him, for her mother, for herself — brought tears to her eyes. She fumbled in her purse for a handkerchief and dabbed at her eyes with it. He avoided watching her until the handkerchief had been put away again.

'I wanted to tell you how it was,' he said. 'All these years, I've wished I could talk to you, or even write. I don't know just what Polly told you, but I've got a pretty good idea. I wanted to be able to tell you that whatever I did — and I'm not excusing it — I did it because I loved your mother, and you.'

She did not trust her voice to reply, and was embarrassed to have to retrieve the handkerchief from her purse.

'I suppose Polly told you I married Elizabeth for the family money?' Nancy nodded briefly. He laughed drily. 'Yes, they said that often enough in the past. But the truth is, Elizabeth and I talked about it from the first. We pretty well knew they'd disinherit her if she married me. I was only a delivery-truck driver, and she . . . well, she was the most beautiful thing that had ever come into my life.'

He paused. Nancy stole a glance, to discover that it was he now who was looking through the window, out to sea. She did not think he was seeing the little sailing boats, though; he was seeing a vision from his past. Her mother, but before she was her mother: when she was his, and his only.

'We married anyway, and we went to Chicago, and they disinherited her. I wish I could say it all worked out happily ever after, but we all know it didn't. I had a job there, but I lost it soon after. I was out of work for a long time. You were born, and things got rougher and rougher. I got another job finally, but there were all those bills, and things piling up, and you got sick for a while, so it was still worse.'

He paused again and when he continued his voice had changed, taken on a new intensity. Nancy had the impression he was begging her to understand the *why* of what he had done.

'One of the fellows I worked with came to me, said he understood I was in a spot over money, and that he and some other friends had an idea how to make some.' He looked directly across the table at her. 'The rest is fairly obvious. I said no at first, and they kept after me, and I began to think of all the things your mother had given up — the luxury she was used to that I couldn't give her, and the money we needed, and the bills, and you . . . and finally I said yes.

'It was all right for a while, until we fouled up on a job. I got away, but the police caught up with me at the apartment. There was some shooting and you woke up terrified. That was when I gave myself up and confessed everything. Anything to spare you and Elizabeth that.'

'I think I remember something, dimly,' she said. 'I've always been afraid of waking up in the darkness. I expect it

44

goes back to that.'

'Probably.' He lit himself another cigarette, giving one to Mick as well. 'That's about all there is,' he said. 'I confessed, pleaded guilty, to keep the trial and the publicity brief. They sent me away. The next thing I heard, your mother was ill; then she died, and I got a letter from Polly saying that she had you and would care for you properly, provided I let you think I was dead. I hated her for it. I could happily have strangled her at the time, but there wasn't anything else I could do, for your sake.' He sounded guilty and sad and even weary.

'But you came now to tell me the truth.'

'I'm an old man. Maybe not in years, but old anyway. I wanted to try to get this straight while I still could.'

'And now?'

He shrugged and said, 'I don't know. We're staying at a little hotel downtown. I thought we'd look around for jobs. I'm not in a hurry to get back to the snows in the east — right, Mick?'

Mick laughed: a thin, hollow sound.

They had finished their coffees. The restaurant was getting crowded and Nancy had seen the waiter casting frequent glances at them.

Her father reached for the check. She did not protest, although she thought his fund of cash was probably not awfully large for the expense of a city like this one.

Now that he had told her what he had come to say, he seemed eager to be gone, as if he were embarrassed. While they had talked some of the furtive air they had displayed before had disappeared; but now it was back, and she saw each of them cast a nervous glance around.

'We'd better go,' her father said. 'It's been nice meeting you after all this time.'

'I hope we can get together again.' She wished she could think of something more to say, some magical grouping of words that would erase all the years and all the strangeness from between them, but nothing came into her mind. They exchanged a few more pleasantries, and then quickly and stealthily the two men were gone, looking fearfully about them, sidling through the crowds of people.

She sat on at the table for a moment, staring after them. Their furtive manner was contagious; she found herself glancing around the room uneasily. *At least,* she thought, *we weren't the only ones holding up a table just for coffee.* Over against the wall a lone man sat at a table, sipping coffee. She thought he had been looking at her when she turned but he quickly dropped his eyes and busied himself with cigarettes and matches.

Something about him seemed familiar. Something about the tilt of his head and ... of course. She had seen him before, on her last flight to San Francisco. He had been wearing a white jacket, and she had seen him later on the street, and thought he was following her.

And now to find him here, in this restaurant, drinking coffee — and watching her?

She decided to leave the room by that route, past his table, so she could get a better look at him. She reached for her purse.

'Beg pardon, miss.' The waiter was just

beside her chair, looking polite but unfriendly. 'Will there be anything else?'

'No, I was just leaving.' She stood and smoothed the front of her cloth coat, but when she turned toward the wall the man she thought was following her was gone. The room was crowded now. She thought she saw him disappearing through the crowd just inside the door, but she couldn't be certain. The waiter cleared his throat, and she smiled at him and moved off, threading her way through the waiting customers and down the steps that led to the street.

No one was obviously waiting for her on the sidewalk or watching for her to come out of the restaurant, but she could not shake an eerie feeling of being watched. But why should anyone want to follow her?

She did not feel like going home. Her father's face kept appearing before her — a blurred superimposition of the one she had just seen across the table and the old face of the photograph.

She got off the cable car and began to walk down toward Chinatown. Almost at once she had moved into another realm of existence. She always had this impression when she came here of having ceased to be of herself and her time, and becoming instead part of another life altogether. The open-fronted shops with their Chinese characters written on the glass, the sea of tan faces framed with jet-black hair, the babble of voices in a singsong language, and the strange scents that assailed her were all foreign to her; and yet because she had known them since childhood, familiar too.

It gave her a queer feeling to realize that the people here were living much as they had lived for centuries. That thought always somehow made the present seem smaller. Seen against a backdrop of centuries, the immediate moment shrank and lost a great deal of significance; and with it shrank the moment's problems.

Today she had met a man who was a stranger to her and yet whose existence, or the presumed lack of it, had greatly influenced her life. He had been torn from her life, but threads had remained to tie them to one another. Yet she could see that they were only threads; and she saw them against the whole fabric of life. Of course, that fabric was only threads, multiplied and added one to the other, and interwoven, but the whole was more than the parts; the colors and turnings of a single strand, insignificant as such, became in the whole a pattern that could not be distinguished until the threads were brought together. Then scenes appeared, flowers bloomed, and one could see that there was a meaning to the whole thing after all.

If there was any significance to what had happened today, to that strained meeting with the man who — by blood at least — was her father, it was not in the single event itself, but in the pattern of which that meeting was a part and which could only be distinguished when all the threads had been brought together. The threads were in the frayed cloth of her mind; she must find the right strands, and bring them together in the right order, to discover the pattern.

'Excuse me, please.' A large woman with a flowered hat emerged from one of the tourist shops along the street bearing a huge folding screen done in vulgar hues that mocked the graceful art of the East. Carrying her purchase to a car parked at the curb, motor running, door open, she stepped directly into Nancy's path, making her stop abruptly.

Someone from behind bumped into her. Nancy turned to apologize to the person but she saw instead another man going by near the curb, skirting the stream of pedestrians that jammed the sidewalk. He had long hair and a beard and he was wearing patched jeans — the same patched jeans he had been wearing when she had seen him before, when he had attacked her in the living room of Aunt Polly's house.

4

It was her assailant, the would-be burglar whose marks she still wore on her throat. He was wearing the same wrap-around sunglasses, so she could not tell if he had seen her or not, but she rather thought not. He gave no sign of it, but strode purposefully along, so determined in his step that even the lady with the folding screen paused to let him past.

Nancy stared after him. What should she do? Certainly she could not go up to him and accuse him of mauling her and trying to rob her aunt's home, but she could hardly just let him disappear in the crowd, either.

She moved back into the stream of people, following the tall man in the patched jeans. She wanted at least to see where he was going so she could report that to the police. She glanced about, trying to fix in her mind her exact location; she had only been wandering before, not paying much attention to where she was.

When she looked back, he had disappeared. She hurried on, looking to the right and left, and came to a break in the shop fronts, a tiny street that went off to the right — no more than an alley, actually, and much too narrow for automotive traffic. Chinatown had many such alleys, rarely explored by the tourists. Mysterious and narrow and shadowy, they seemed to beckon the adventurous. Here, behind doors that were usually closed, was the real world of the 'town'. At little tables artisans worked, some creating junk for the cheap tourists' shops, others patiently carving out little works of art. Behind other doors people lived much as their ancestors had lived. Sometimes one strolled these alleys and caught the scent of opium being smoked in a pipe by a wizened old man who dreamed of an old world, an old way of life that faded like the smoke from his pipe — so ephemeral now that the smoker might wonder if it had existed at all, or if he had only dreamed it in his pipe-dreams.

She paused at the entry to the alley. It

seemed empty, but a short way beyond another alley branched off it, and she thought she heard the distant echo of footsteps. She stepped into the alley and was at once separated from the crowds behind her as if she had stepped out of time.

A short distance along, a door stood open, and inside a group of men, all dressed in the old style, were drinking tea. They paused, their high, ringing chatter falling silent as she passed by. Foolishly, she remembered stories she had heard as a child about mysterious and wicked things that went on here — men shanghaied to work the ships waiting in the harbor; young women stolen away to serve in brothels in faraway cities of the East. But that was all in the past — wasn't it?

She came to where the other alley branched off. She saw no one, but this alley too went only for a few yards before it turned. She heard a gentle tinkling of wind chimes in a doorway and further away, incongruously, a radio playing acid rock music. She was frightened, not by anything in particular, but by the atmosphere, by the old stories, by the sight of the bearded man — even a little by the meeting with her father, and his furtive way of looking over her shoulder. She had an urge to look over her shoulder just now.

She knew that kind of fear. She had seen stewardesses fall victim to it: a nameless fear that started with some unlucky incident and built with the tensions normal to any job; and in the end the simple banking of a plane — an ordinary, safe thing — would terrify her as if they had suddenly spun out of control.

She did not mean to succumb to it, to become hysterical. This second alley, she reasoned, and the little one branching off it, would surely take her through to Grant, the main thoroughfare. Her strange man with the beard had disappeared, no doubt into one of the many closed doorways she had passed. It only proved that she was not cut out to be a detective.

She started along the second alleyway, hurrying. She had a feeling of eyes watching her and told herself that was only another trick of the mind, trying to frighten her into succumbing to fear.

There was a sound to her left. Her heart jumped. The bearded man had waited for her in a doorway. Quite casually, as if this were some prearranged meeting, he stepped out into the alley, blocking her path.

She moved in a futile attempt to evade the hands reaching for her, but it was all too unexpected. He seized her, grabbing her wrist violently and yanking her toward him. She felt a shudder of terror go up her spine and she tried to scream, but his other hand clapped over her mouth so that nothing came out but one short squeal of fright.

They scuffled together for a moment, making no sound but the faint grating of their shoes on the pavement. It was like some ancient Oriental mime-dance, all movement and stance, with no music or voices. Only it was real, that hand trying to get a hold on her throat — and this time he would not go away and leave her unconscious, she was sure.

'Hey, what's going on?'

It was a man's voice behind them. She heard footsteps running toward them.

Suddenly her assailant whirled her around. She had a glimpse of a man coming at them before she was flung forward, hard, into his arms. She stumbled and fell against him, and the two of them almost went down.

He regained his balance and steadied her, and she felt a strong, sure arm about her. She gasped for breath, feeling the trembling gradually subside in her shoulders.

'That man . . . ' she tried to say, and her voice broke.

'Easy; don't worry about it. He's gone now.'

She looked back over her shoulder. 'Gone?'

'Took off when I came up. Guess he figured two of us was more than he wanted to handle. Are you all right?'

'Yes, thank you.' Growing calmer now, she became aware of the feel of his arms about her. Gently she freed herself from his embrace and took a step back, looking up into his face.

'What are you doing here, anyway?' she asked, her voice still a little unsteady.

He chuckled and said, 'I was about to ask you the same thing. Actually I was just wandering around, sightseeing, and that little alley back there looked interesting — you know, the mysteries of the Orient, that sort of thing. I started along it and I thought I heard someone cry out. I came to investigate and found you and your boyfriend wrestling with one another. Now how did you get here, and who was he?'

'I don't know who he is. I was just sightseeing myself and King Kong pounced on me from that doorway.' She was trying to sound flippant and unconcerned, not altogether sure why she didn't want to tell this man the truth. Perhaps it was because he wasn't telling the truth, either. The possibility, however, that he was just strolling along and happened to hear her cry was a bit too thick, considering how often he had been close by the last day or so. She had seen him just a short while ago, at the same restaurant in which she had sat with her father and Mick. And yesterday she was sure he had been following her.

Now, here he was in Chinatown, in time to save her from an attacker, and she simply could not accept that it was mere coincidence. He was watching her. He did not believe her either, she thought; but he had decided, apparently, not to challenge her explanation.

'You still look a little shaky,' he said, smiling. 'How about a drink somewhere?'

She hesitated only briefly. 'All right,' she said, taking a deep breath. She had a feeling that things had worked out altogether right for him. He had wanted to meet her and ask her for a drink, and not for the obvious reasons either. On the other hand, she was curious about him, too. She had no idea who he was or why he was following her. He had rather a rugged face, of strong, even harsh lines and features; and when he took her arm, as he did now to escort her out of the alley, his grip was firm but surprisingly gentle.

'I'm Tom Farroday, by the way,' he said. 'From Seattle. A visitor to your city.'

'I'm Nancy Dunbar. And what makes you think it's my city? I could be a tourist too, couldn't I?'

'You just seem at home in the city. How about that place over there?'

'I'm sure it will be fine,' she said, amused at his attempt to change the subject. He had slipped up in announcing that he knew she was familiar with the city, which he oughtn't to have known if he had just seen her for the first time in that alley. 'I live in Los Angeles, actually, but San Francisco is home — sort of.'

'What does that mean, sort of?'

'I was born in Chicago. It's a long story, I'm afraid.

'I'm in town on business for two full weeks.'

'What sort of business?'

He hesitated for a second or two. 'That's another long story.'

'I'm in town for a full month.'

'Touché,' he said with a laugh.

They passed through a red-painted door cut in the shape of a circle, trying to adjust their eyes to the dim light. The interior was done in red and black and fake bamboo, and a dozen or more sets of wind chimes jangled with every breeze.

A maître d' approached and when they

declined lunch, led them to a little table in the bar. Except for the bartender and a waitress wearing what must have been intended as a mini-kimono, they had the place to themselves. They waited quietly until the girl had brought their drinks — a vermouth for her, Scotch for him.

'What sort of work do you do?' she asked.

'I'm in insurance.'

'Oh.' She gave a little laugh. 'I was trying to guess, and I had you categorized in something rough and dangerous.'

'Will it help if I assure you that policy-holders sometimes get violent?'

They laughed together, becoming more at ease with one another. 'Miss Dunbar,' he began, and then paused. 'It is 'miss', isn't it?'

'Ms. But you can call me Nancy. And no, there isn't any husband or fiancé.'

'Well, you don't have to worry either; there's no wife or mistress who's going to come screaming through the door any minute intent on pulling your hair out. And call me Tom, please . . . ' He hesitated. 'Why don't you show me a little of the city while I'm here? I could use a guide.'

One little part of her mind was trying to warn her of something. This was not just a casual flirtation. Their meeting had not been the accident it had seemed. He had wanted to meet her — had been following her in order to arrange it — and not, surely, because her beauty had bewitched him.

However, it was impossible to heed the little warning voices when he smiled at her like that, and when he said, 'Why don't we start with dinner this evening?'

She nodded. 'I'd love to.'

5

The restaurant they went to was high up on a hillside with a spectacular view of the bay. The house had once been a base for smugglers and it still had an aura of romance and adventure.

Nancy turned to look at the view beyond the window. It was twilight and San Francisco was donning her evening dress. Lights twinkled everywhere against the bluish-gray of evening, and the water of the bay reflected a galaxy of lights back at them in twinkling profusion.

'I always find San Francisco enchanting,' she said. 'It's so out of step with the parade, if you know what I mean.'

'I thought you were practically a native. You talk like you really are just a visitor.'

'I told you, it's a long story.'

'I'm in no hurry. Start with Chicago.'

She laughed, but she did begin to talk, of Chicago when she was a child. She only meant to tell him the bare outline, omitting the emotional parts and the business about her father, and her unhappiness at losing both her parents so close together. But somehow words came that she hadn't meant to speak and she found herself telling him everything, as she had never done with anyone else before, and his gentle encouragement made it easy for her to unburden herself. And no matter what she said, even when she became a little maudlin as she spoke of her meeting with her father, he seemed to understand.

By the time she had finished her story, they had finished their dinner. 'Good heavens,' she said, leaning back in her chair with a cup of strong black coffee in her hands, 'I've talked for hours. You must have thought you were at a lecture on how a girl grows up lonely.'

'It was fascinating. Although it's still incredible to me that a girl as beautiful as you could ever be lonely or feel unloved.'

'Well, there are different kinds of love. Some sorts I've been offered often enough.'

'Yes, most men would want to make a

pass,' he admitted, signaling the waiter for their check.

'But you didn't.'

'I haven't yet,' he said with a mock-warning look.

It was night when they came out of the restaurant. She had worn a full skirt in a below-the-knee length, and a gaucho shirt, and she carried a shawl for protection against the city's night-time coolness. She slipped the shawl about her shoulders now.

The attendant brought his car around — a Jaguar sports car, incredibly long and low-looking. The throaty rumble of the engine echoed back from the hills. 'Want the top up?' Tom asked.

'And waste all this delicious night? Not on your life.' She fixed the shawl so it covered her hair and fell over her shoulders, and they started down the curving street into the city.

'Is anyone waiting up for you?'

'I hope not.'

'Shall we make a night of it?'

'I'd like to,' she said simply.

He smiled and shifted gears as they

turned a corner. She gave him directions to a nightspot she had in mind. At the same time, another part of her mind had gone back to his question, whether anyone was waiting up for her.

She suspected Aunt Polly might be. Not that Aunt Polly was in the habit of checking her comings and goings, but she was in the habit of finishing any discussion she became engaged in, and she and Nancy had been engaged in one which Nancy's departure for this date had left unfinished.

The discussion had bordered dangerously upon being a quarrel. Earlier in the day, Tom had insisted upon driving Nancy home and Aunt Polly, who normally did not watch for glimpses of Nancy's escorts, had been at a window, had seen him, and asked casually enough who he was.

Nancy had told her quite frankly of meeting him earlier; of seeing their burglar and following him; of being accosted and rescued by Mr. Farroday. She told her aunt as well of her conviction that Tom had been following her in an attempt to meet her.

To her surprise, Aunt Polly had reacted rather strongly to the story. 'My dear niece, you can't tell what this man may have in mind to do,' she said in a stern voice.

'Well, if he were planning bodily harm, it seems unlikely he would have rescued me from that other man. And I can't think what other dangers there could be.'

'There's no end to things. People nowadays do awful things with no discernible motive or logic to them. And the fact that he saved you from somebody else doesn't mean he means you no harm. Maybe he wanted to be certain he was the one who inflicted it.'

'He had the perfect opportunity to do so and wasted it.'

Aunt Polly, who had been sitting, stood and stretched herself to her full height. 'I do not think you should keep your date with the gentleman,' she said. 'I think that you should let me deal with him.'

'But I can't do that,' Nancy said firmly. 'I've promised to show him the city, and I mean to keep my promise. And frankly, whatever mysterious motives he might have, I liked him. I enjoyed being with him and I'm looking forward to seeing him again, and if he strangles me while we're dancing I will never get to hear you say, 'I told you so'.'

Her stubbornness on the subject surprised Aunt Polly. In fact, it surprised Nancy herself. Afterward, feeling that she had spoken a bit strongly, she took her aunt's hand and patted it gently.

'Aunt, I've done a lot of travelling and I've met many men. I think I'm pretty good at sizing them up. Please don't worry yourself needlessly about Mr. Farroday.'

Polly gave a sigh. 'I've often wondered if it was right to encourage you to be so independent.'

'You wouldn't want me clinging helplessly to you all the time, would you?' She laughed a little; they both knew her aunt would definitely not want that.

'You haven't said a word about your father,' Aunt Polly said, changing the subject abruptly.

Nancy launched into that subject,

describing how her father had looked and sounded, while avoiding the more personal aspects of their conversation. She knew that her aunt sensed she was holding back, but Aunt Polly did not press her, for which Nancy was grateful.

She thought the discussion of Tom Farroday was ended, but later, when Nancy came down to go out, her aunt had been seated with a book, giving every indication of devoting an evening to it.

'I'll see you when you come in,' she said pointedly.

'There's no need to wait up.' But Nancy supposed after all that her aunt would be waiting up, to insure that Mr. Farroday had not taken an axe to her.

'Park anyplace along here.' They were in North Beach area. San Francisco is a city composed of many ethnic groups, each in their own neighborhood, which spill over into one another. North Beach is known for its Italian restaurants and cafés — and for its nightlife.

They found a parking place finally. There was some difficulty with a couple in a large sedan with out-of-state license plates who came up behind them with horn blasting to announce that they wanted the parking space, and thought they ought to be given it. Not intimidated, Tom whipped the agile Jaguar around the bulky fenders of the sedan and into the parking space.

They walked the few blocks to the club Nancy had suggested for a starting point. At The Bocce Ball, regular entertainers performed operatic numbers, often assisted by waiters and bartenders and even, sometimes, patrons. It was a popular nightspot here among the people of Italian descent, many of whom were raised from childhood on Verdi and Puccini.

As the waiter led them to a table, a soprano sang 'Dove Sono' from *The Marriage of Figaro*, about a past that has fled and cannot be recaptured.

Something of my past has fled, Nancy thought, though she was not altogether sure she would have wanted to recapture it if she could. Her glance went to her companion, and her pulse quickened ever so slightly. It was the future that interested her now.

Not for anything would she have missed that evening. They sat and listened to the music of the operatic masters, and sipped wine. Then, an abrupt change of pace, they went to a crowded little club to dance to the loud music of a rock group. Afterward, once more in the Jaguar, they had sped through the night to the Golden Gate Bridge. From a view terrace on its opposite end, they stood and watched the fog creeping in over the city until the lights had become dim candles flickering beyond the mist.

They finished at another dance spot, this one quiet and elegant with soft, old-fashioned-sounding music that invited close dancing and whispered remarks. They drove home by way of Fisherman's Wharf, busy and loud during the day, but now asleep and ghostly, musing over its own colorful past. They got out of the car to stand by the water for a while, watching the gentle undulations and the occasional startled leap of a wave, surprised from its sleep by a passing fish.

It was nearly three when he brought her to the front door of the little mansion. Far from tired, she felt buoyant and eager, as if she were walking on air.

He kissed her, only once, and that briefly. She ran up the stairs singing softly to herself, her head spinning. She let herself in quietly so as not to disturb her aunt. She needn't have bothered, however. Aunt Polly was still sitting in the darkened living room.

'Nancy, is that you?' she called.

'Yes.' Nancy went to the door and clicked on the light. 'What on earth are you doing still up, and sitting in the dark?'

'I wanted to see that you got home all right,' her aunt said, crossly, 'and I got tired of the light.' She looked, Nancy thought with alarm, beside herself. It was hard to imagine that her aunt, who after all had never had any profound affection for her, should be so frightfully worried over her welfare at this late stage of the game, but her aunt looked like a woman driven almost to hysteria with worry. It was the sort of emotional strain Nancy, as a stewardess, was trained to watch for, and she knew that the only way to cope with it, if it was to be coped with, was with deliberate calm.

'Well, now that you can see for yourself that all my limbs are still intact, perhaps you ought to think of going to bed.'

Polly jumped to her feet, eyes flashing hotly. 'This is not something to joke about. I absolutely forbid you to see this Mr. Farroday again.'

Nancy was shocked into a momentary speechlessness. Her impulse was to remind her aunt that she was a grown woman and could see whomever she chose. Her sympathy for her aunt's state of mind caused her to keep that thought to herself, however. Instead, she said, 'Let's discuss it in the morning, shall we?'

'There is nothing to discuss,' Polly declared, her voice rising shrilly. 'This is my house and I — '

Suddenly she clasped a hand to her breast. Her eyes rolled upward in her head and a grimace of pain flashed across her face, distorting it cruelly. As suddenly as if she had been struck a blow from behind, she fell forward in a faint.

At once Nancy sprang forward, stooping beside her aunt's fallen figure. She checked the pulse and found it weak. Fortunately her aunt's longtime physician, Doctor Williams, lived nearby and, perhaps because Polly had been generous in helping him get his practice started, he coddled her to a great extent. So although it was late, Nancy did not hesitate to run to the phone and call him on his home number.

His housekeeper answered, and after a show of reluctance went to summon the doctor. A minute later his familiar voice was on the line. 'I'll be right there,' he said when Nancy had explained.

To her surprise, Ellen seemed not at all surprised when Nancy summoned her. 'Again,' she said. She got up and donned a robe and came down the stairs with Nancy.

Doctor Williams was there in less than five minutes, wearing an old raincoat over his pajamas and carrying his familiar black bag.

The three of them moved Polly to her

bed. It was obvious to Nancy that Ellen and Doctor Williams had been through this before and that for the moment at least her help was not needed. She stepped into the hall while they tended to her aunt. She that saw Doctor Williams was preparing a syringe as she went out, and supposed that he knew what the difficulty was and had treated it before.

In a short while the doctor came out of the bedroom, closing the door softly. 'She'll be all right,' he said. 'I've given her something to make her sleep, and Ellen will stay with her for a little while.'

'Doctor Williams,' Nancy said, 'is this something that has happened regularly? Is my aunt ill?'

He gave her a surprised look. 'You mean she hasn't told you?'

Nancy shook her head. 'Told me what?'

'Of course it isn't really my place to tell you, and yet . . . ' He hesitated, and seemed to reach a decision. 'Your aunt is a very sick woman,' he said. Something in his tone seemed to Nancy to imply more than he was saying.

'How sick?'

Again he hesitated before answering, 'Fatally. I've given her a few months to live. A year at the most. I should have thought she would have told you.'

★　★　★

Although Nancy felt certain that sleep would never come, she slept almost at once after going to bed. It was midmorning when she woke, still a little tired. The day before had been incredibly crowded with events. Now she had a new circumstance to adjust herself to — her aunt's sickness.

Of course everyone dies and one might as well accept it, but surely no one was ever quite ready for it. If there had not been any deep warmth of feeling between herself and her aunt, she was truly fond of Aunt Polly and grateful that the woman had taken her in and cared for her to the best of her abilities. She could not but be deeply moved by the news of Aunt Polly's illness.

She'd had to talk herself out of a slight feeling of guilt. It was the scene with her that had precipitated Aunt Polly's attack last night. The doctor had assured her, however, that it was not the first such attack and that they were likely to be brought on by almost anything.

'Whenever your aunt gets herself worked up, which she's going to be increasingly likely to do, whatever you say or do, she's likely to have one of these spells,' Doctor Williams told her.

There was something more that was troubling her, though, and that was the nature of the disagreement that had led up to the faint. Granted, Aunt Polly might be under a strain and likely to be irritable, but the scene was so unlike anything that had ever occurred in the past that Nancy thought there must be more to it than she had at first realized.

She could not believe that her aunt was suddenly becoming possessive or overly protective, nor could she accept the idea that her aunt's emotional state of the previous night sprang from concern because Nancy was out with a strange man. Aunt Polly was anything but Victorian, after all.

There was the question, too, of why

Tom Farroday had been so interested in her before even meeting her that he had followed her about the city for two days until he had met her.

She tried to think if there might be some connection between the two oddities — Tom Farroday's unexplained interest in her, and her aunt's alarm over Tom Farroday. She could not think of any links that connected the two.

As to her own feelings, she could not help what had happened between herself and Tom. She had fallen unexpectedly and inescapably in love with him.

The phone rang. The ringing ceased almost at once, and she knew Ellen had answered it. Nancy lay in bed for a few minutes more.

Ellen tapped at the door and poked her head inside long enough to say, 'Telephone.' Tom's voice wished her a cheerful good morning.

'I only wish it were,' she said gloomily. She told him briefly of what had transpired since she had seen him. 'You don't know my aunt, do you?' she finished.

'You mean have I ever met her? No.

Look, I'll stop by a little later, all right?'

'I'm not sure . . . '

'You'll have to have lunch anyway,' he said, before she could finish her objection, 'and you sound as if you could use some cheering up.'

'All right. Say, at eleven? I'll meet you in front.' She did not want to risk her aunt's reaction to bringing Tom Farroday directly into the house, at least until she could get clear in her own mind what her aunt's real objection to him was. She dressed and freshened up before going to see Aunt Polly, determined to put a good face on things.

Ellen was just emerging from Aunt Polly's bedroom, bearing a breakfast tray.

'How is she?' Nancy asked.

'Well enough to be cantankerous,' Ellen said. 'Will you be having breakfast?'

'Just some coffee, I think. I'll come down to the kitchen for it.'

Aunt Polly was propped up in bed on a mountain of pillows. Despite her pallor, she looked positively ferocious, nor did her look soften when it fastened on her niece.

'I suppose that fool of a doctor has been blabbing everything he knows,' she said sharply.

'He told me of your condition.'

'Well, we may as well have things straight, then. I'm not afraid of dying. We're all dying, from the moment we're born, moving toward the moment of death. It comes sooner or later, that's all. When it comes, I can tolerate it. But I cannot tolerate a lot of sniffling and mumbling and hand-wringing, and if you have any idea of behaving like that, you might as well pack up your things now and clear out. Is that understood?'

'Yes, Aunt,' Nancy said somberly. Then, because she could not help but be amazed at her aunt's reaction to what anyone else would view as a tragedy, she added, 'You are incorrigible.'

Aunt Polly's reply was an untranslatable snort.

'Furthermore, I have decided to stay here with you. I'm going to ask the airlines for a leave of absence.'

'That isn't at all necessary,' Polly Dunbar said vehemently. 'I've told you I won't tolerate a lot of hand-wringing and that sort of thing.'

'You'll need someone here with you as . . . as things move along.'

'I have Ellen. And the doctor assures me there will not be any great pain or discomfort until near the end. I shall then have a full-time nurse brought in, someone professionally trained. You would only be a nuisance, Nancy.'

Nancy started to press the issue and then thought better of it. Surely her aunt had a right to have things as she wanted them. But, Nancy told herself, neither did she mean to be thrust away, out of the picture. She was fond of her aunt and she knew that, in her own way, Aunt Polly cared for her, and she could not help but feel certain that, nearer the end, Aunt Polly would welcome the nearness of someone who cared.

Aloud, she said, 'Is there anything you want? I'm going out for lunch.'

'With that Farroday fellow, I suppose?'

'Yes. Would you like to meet him? He's really quite a pleasant man.'

Aunt Polly drew herself up sternly, as if

her niece had made an off-color remark. 'Indeed I would not. I am not in the habit of having strange men traipsing about in my bedroom. For all I know, he may be looking the place over preparatory to robbing it.'

Nancy only laughed and said, 'If you think of anything, let me know.'

She had coffee and a piece of toast in the kitchen. It was difficult to think of her aunt as being fatally ill when the older woman stubbornly refused to act as a woman in those circumstances might be expected to act. Nancy made a mental note to talk to Doctor Williams further as to what to expect as the time drew nearer, and whether it would be advisable for her to stay.

Ellen, in answer to a question of Nancy's, said, 'It's eerie, isn't it, how she's taken it? I thought at first she was just putting up a brave front, and a couple of times I even cried because she sounded so heroic, but eventually I came to see she meant just what she said; she didn't feel sorry for herself and she didn't want anyone else feeling sorry for her either.

She's made up her mind to it, and that's all there is to it. After a time, you get used to the idea. If she was carrying on herself, it would be different, but now that you know, and you see how it is, you'll get over the first shock and it won't be so bad then.'

'I suppose you're right.' Nancy started from the room, pausing at the door to say, 'I'm expecting a gentleman by. If he comes while I'm upstairs, show him into the parlor, won't you?'

Ellen said, almost as an aside, 'Things will be different after your aunt goes, won't they?'

'In what way do you mean?'

'There'll be scores of men hanging around then, only they'll be after the money, most of them. A rich girl never knows whether a man likes her for herself or only for her money. Well, at least you know that's not the case with this one.'

6

Ellen turned back to the pot she was stirring on the stove. As Nancy went up the stairs, she could not help but think of what Ellen had just said. It had not occurred to her before that she would indeed become an heiress when her aunt died. They had never discussed the subject at any length, but several years before Aunt Polly had made a new will, and had at the time explained that it had been done to provide for Nancy.

'I had no relatives before, and so everything had been left to charity,' Aunt Polly had explained. 'But now that I have a relative, it seemed pointless to allow that to remain as it was.'

Nancy had not pointed out that her aunt had always had relatives — she and her mother and even her father had been there before, in Chicago. She supposed that during that time, in Aunt Polly's mind they had not existed at all.

Ellen's remark about Tom Farroday crept into Nancy's thoughts. It was true, he could not know about the money, and so that could not affect his interest in her — could it? He had been following her about the city, true; for some reason he had been very set on meeting her. But that was not because she was due to become a wealthy heiress, was it?

She could not see how he possibly could have known of this. She knew of no connection between him and, say, Ellen, or Doctor Williams, nor did she have any idea who else would know of both her aunt's illness, and of her aunt's will.

Yet, Tom had 'arranged' their meeting, almost, and the question of why was still unanswered.

These thoughts so clouded her mind that she was distracted and unresponsive during their lunch. She could not bring herself to bluntly ask some of the questions she was pondering. If he were completely innocent of any but the obvious interest in her, her questions could not help but turn him against her and she did not want to do that. At least, she would give romance a chance.

Whatever his thoughts were about her aloofness, however, he kept them pretty much to himself. They had lunch in a quaint little tea shop and while they ate, he kept up an impersonal conversation. He did not seem to notice, or to mind, that he was to a large extent carrying her end of it as well as his own.

Later, when he brought her back to the house, she tried to apologize. 'I'm afraid I was rather out of it today,' she said. 'And I am sorry.'

'You don't have to apologize to me. I understand that you're preoccupied with your aunt's illness, which is as it should be.'

'Thank you, for not making any demands just now.'

'I will make one, though. How about dinner?'

She hesitated for a moment. 'Let's make it tomorrow evening, shall we? I doubt that Aunt Polly will welcome my company, but I feel I really should keep this evening open.'

She was surprised on going in to find

Aunt Polly seated in the parlor reading a book of poetry, which she put aside with a faint air of reluctance. 'I'm surprised to see you up and about,' Nancy said.

'I hope you did not expect me to behave like a helpless invalid,' Aunt Polly said. 'I warned you that you needn't expect a lot of lying abed and groaning. I'm going shopping tomorrow, as a matter of fact.'

'Do you think that's wise? It might be dangerous to exert yourself.'

'Dangerous?' Aunt Polly lifted an eyebrow. 'What might it do — kill me?'

Nancy was shocked into silence by the bluntness of the remark. Yet she could see that the question was unanswerable. Husbanding her strength could not much alter the course of events for her aunt. She could be cautious and conserve her physical resources, or she could live her life exactly as she had been living it; either way the sickness that was growing within her would continue to grow, and would have its way with her, and she would die. Whichever path she chose, it would lead to the same destination.

It seemed after all that there was nothing to be gained by her efforts to watch over her aunt. Polly seemed determined not to be watched over and steadfastly insisted that she hoped her niece would not plan on staying for an extended visit. 'Although,' she added, 'this is your home, of course, and I would hardly refuse to let you stay.'

A bit later, as if realizing that she might have been more than a little ruthless in dealing with the matter, she said, more kindly, 'If you have nothing to do tomorrow, you might go shopping with me. If, that is, you don't act every moment as if you expect me to keel over in my tracks.'

'Perhaps I shall. I'll see.' The subject of Tom Farroday, which had brought about the latest crisis in her aunt's health, seemed to have been dropped as a subject for discussion.

As it turned out, she did not after all go shopping with Aunt Polly. During the evening, which she did spend quietly with her aunt, Nancy received a call from her father. Trying not to mind Aunt Polly's disapproving look, Nancy went to the telephone to talk to him. She wished she could put a note of enthusiastic happiness into her voice, which she knew sounded guarded and hesitant.

'I thought maybe we could get together for lunch again,' he said when they had exchanged greetings.

'Yes, I'd like that. Tomorrow?' They made their arrangements. She asked if he had had the opportunity to see any of the sights, and when she learned that he had not, she suggested a car.

'I can pick you up at eleven, and we can drive over to Sausalito by way of the Golden Gate Bridge.'

'I don't want to cause any trouble,' he said doubtfully. The note of uncertainty in his voice had the effect of removing her own.

'No trouble,' she said more firmly. 'I'll be by at eleven, then.'

Aunt Polly was scowling when Nancy came back to her chair. 'This is really most inconvenient,' she said. 'I had counted on your going shopping with me tomorrow, and now it seems you'll be traipsing off to lunch with your father instead.'

Surprised, Nancy said, 'I didn't think it mattered greatly whether I did or didn't go shopping with you tomorrow. But I can call my father back and make other arrangements if it matters. I'm sure that it will be all the same to him if we have dinner instead.'

'Oh, let it be. I'm only being cross. There's no particular need of your assistance tomorrow.

'I don't mind making other arrangements,' Nancy said, but Aunt Polly would not hear of it.

'If the truth be known, I suppose I'm just being difficult because I disapprove of that man, still. But you've every right to see him if you wish. He is your father, as far as that goes.'

She closed up her book, signifying that the conversation too was closed, and prepared to go up to bed. When she had gone, Nancy found herself puzzling over her aunt's strange behavior. She had never known her aunt to interfere in what she did with her personal life, or even to take any great interest in it. Now, within a matter of a day, they had quarreled over Tom Farroday and had come close to one over lunch between Nancy and her father.

She could only assume this was part of her aunt's condition. It was sad to think of that eminently calm woman turning into a hypersensitive and over-emotional person. She made a note to ask Doctor Williams about this.

On her way from the room, her eyes fell on the case containing the jade figurines. She shivered involuntarily, remembering the burglar. Aunt Polly had not mentioned whether she had heard anything from the police. She supposed it was unlikely they would find the man with so little to go on and realized belatedly that she should have told them she had seen the man in Chinatown. Perhaps something so seemingly trivial would be the very clue they would need to track him down.

Another thought crossed her mind. No one had contacted her for a description of the burglar. So much had happened to her since that the lack of police activity had not occurred to her until now. Her aunt had friends in City Hall in a manner of speaking. She wondered if perhaps someone shouldn't be chided. Granted, crime rates were high, and the police had their hands full, but surely a burglary and an assault justified at least a visit from an officer, if only to make the victim feel that justice was being sought.

'Or perhaps,' she thought aloud, going up the stairs, 'Aunt Polly gave them the description of the man when she reported the incident.'

She paused on the steps. But Aunt Polly hadn't known the man's description. True, Nancy had described him to her, but that was later, after the police had been called and the incident reported.

She went up and, seeing a light at her aunt's door, tapped softly and went in. Polly was in bed. She gave Nancy a questioning look.

'I was only wondering,' Nancy said, 'about the police. They haven't been around to question me about that burglary the other day.'

'Attempted burglary,' Aunt Polly corrected her.

'Attempted burglary, then. But they still haven't been around.'

'There's a very good reason. I did not report it to them.'

'But you said . . . '

'I know I said that I had. You were all excited, and it seemed best to pacify you. But the truth was, I just saw no benefit from all those strange men trooping around the place, getting underfoot.'

Nancy was aghast. 'But a crime had been committed.'

'Only an attempted crime. Nothing was taken.'

'I was knocked unconscious.'

'Yes, and that's quite unfortunate. But after all, you weren't truly harmed. You've been as spry as ever since then, leading me to believe that the damage was minimal. As for getting the police involved, I still don't see that that would have accomplished anything.'

'I don't know what to say,' Nancy said, shaking her head.

'Then I suggest good night. It's late

and I'm a bit fatigued. And there's no need to work yourself up over this business. If you read the papers at all, you must know people are breaking into houses everywhere, a dozen a minute. I doubt that the police would have paid much attention if we had called them. No harm was done. Except for making a report, there's little they could do. Think of that description you gave me of the man — there must be a million young men around who would fit it.'

'I suppose you're right,' Nancy said reluctantly. 'But I did see him again.'

'A chance in a million. And you would recognize him if you saw him, but the police might not. No, I think we'd only have gotten ourselves a lot of bother for nothing.'

In the soft comfort of her own bed, however, Nancy could not help her thoughts going back to the memory of that man's arms about her, his hands at her throat. It was still terrifyingly vivid, as was her fright at meeting him face-to-face again in a Chinatown alley.

Suppose he came back? After all, he

had not gotten what he came for; might he not return?

* * *

She came down in the morning to find Ellen rushing about all in a dither.

'It's my sister, Rose,' Ellen declared over her shoulder while fussing with her handbag. 'The one in Monterey. Some man just called to tell me she was in a dreadful accident and has been taken to the hospital.'

'How awful,' Nancy exclaimed. 'Shall I drive you down there?'

'Thank you, no, that won't be necessary. I can make a good bus connection if I hurry.' She rushed back to her room for something she had forgotten. 'There's my taxi now,' she said as she ran back down the stairs. 'I'll call tomorrow.' With that she was gone.

The morning was warm. Nancy found her aunt in the breakfast room, the windows open on the little garden outside. A bee noisily explored some potted geraniums on the windowsill, and a gentle breeze brought the familiar ocean scent of the city inside.

'Poor Ellen,' Nancy said, pouring herself some coffee.

Aunt Polly asked absent-mindedly, 'Why do you say that?'

'Because of her sister,' Nancy said a bit sharply. 'It's an unpleasant thing to go through. Not everyone is as stoic about death as you.'

'Yes, that's true,' Aunt Polly said quickly, as if she had been far away in her thoughts. 'I'm sorry if I sounded unsympathetic.'

Nancy studied her aunt surreptitiously. She did not believe the Aunt Polly was at all sorry or sympathetic. Something other than Ellen was on her mind. She had a look in her eyes that was . . . Nancy paused, trying to think of the right word. Calculating, perhaps. And beneath that, something that touched a responsive chord deep within Nancy's own psyche, something of fear or anxiety. Some premonition of disaster stirred along the base of Nancy's spine, and she shivered.

'Are you cold?' Aunt Polly asked. 'I can

close the window.'

'No, no. I was only thinking.'

She was still thinking later when, dressed for lunch, she went to the garage for one of the two cars her aunt kept there. Her aunt was already gone, and the Bentley with her.

Nancy had agreed to pick up her father outside his small residential hotel. She climbed into the more mundane Chevrolet and backed out of the garage.

She found the little hotel with no difficulty, but her father was not waiting outside as they had agreed. Puzzled, she searched for a parking space and walked back to the hotel. When she inquired at the desk, she found that Mr. Blair had gone out perhaps fifteen minutes ago. No, the thin little man behind the desk answered her question, there was no message for her.

'What about the other gentleman?' Nancy asked, realizing she did not know Mickey's last name.

'You just missed him. He went out just a few minutes ago.'

Nancy was puzzled by her father's

failure to keep their date, and hurt more than she wished to admit to herself. She felt utterly crushed with shame. She drove around the city because she could not bear to be still. She wished she had been braver when she had met him; simpler and more open. She might have told him what her experience of loneliness had been, and what it had been like not feeling that she belonged anywhere or to anyone.

She discovered that she had driven through the military reservation that was the Presidio, and was on the narrow road that ran down to Land's End. She drove to where it ended in an unpaved parking area, by an old brick fort intended to guard the bay, though it had never been used. The Golden Gate Bridge arched overhead. Here at its base she was at the water's edge, and could watch the waves lashing violently against the rocks below. Something within her seemed to recognize and respond to their angry surge.

After a time she felt calmer. She could tell herself, without having to quite believe it, that her father had some very reasonable and utterly unavoidable reason for not keeping their date, and when she arrived home it would be to discover that he had left a message which had only just missed her when she went out.

She remembered then that the house was empty — her aunt was out, and Ellen was in Monterey. So he really might have tried to reach her and been unable to do so. Perhaps he was trying to call right now, to apologize, and the phone was ringing gloomily because it knew from the stillness of the house that no one would answer its summons.

There was no urgent ringing of the telephone as she let herself back into the house. She came dispiritedly into the living room and paused just inside the doorway, staring at the broken case where the green men had stood that morning; at the glass scattered upon the carpet.

They jade figurines were gone.

7

She had a sudden impression of déjà vu and whirled about, almost expecting to see again the man trying to steal from the house behind her; but this time there was nothing there. This time he had come, had gotten what he came for, and had gone. She was glad not to have to confront him again. But she thought at once of her aunt, already burdened with the knowledge of approaching death. And of all her possessions, none mattered as much to her as did the green men. Surely it would break her failing heart to learn that they were gone.

★   ★   ★

Aunt Polly took it rather better than she had expected. She arrived close on the heels of the policemen themselves, coming into the room while Nancy was still trying to explain to the plainclothes man in charge.

Aunt Polly paused in the doorway, much as her niece had done a short time before, and surveyed the room with a flick of her eyes, bringing them to rest on Nancy. 'The green men have been taken,' she said, making it not a question, but a statement of what was obvious even at a glance. Nancy only nodded.

'Who are you?' the detective asked.

She scarcely looked at him. 'I am Polly Dunbar, and this is my home. Have you arrested the man yet?'

'No,' he said, a little cowed by her manner.

'Do you know who he is?' She removed her gloves carefully, one at a time, placing them neatly on a table, and took off her hat. She had been to her hairdresser's again and looked very smart and well bred, and quite in control of herself.

The detective assumed a shrewd look. 'How do you know it was a man?'

'Because I doubt that a koala bear did all this.'

'And he's been here before,' Nancy added.

The detective turned on her. 'He's

someone you know?'

'Not exactly.' Nancy hesitated. She had seen the fiercely disapproving look her aunt had turned on her, but it was too late now. And anyway, it seemed to her that the police ought to know about that other time. For one thing, she could describe the thief, and she couldn't do that without explaining the previous incident.

'Someone broke in before,' she went on, avoiding her aunt's gaze. 'I came in and caught him in the act, in a manner of speaking. He knocked me unconscious and then escaped.'

'Without taking anything?'

'Yes. We — that is, I assumed he was after the green men and that my appearance threw him off, so to speak, so that he panicked and ran.'

'What are these green men, anyway?' The detective had decided he did not like the older woman and he did not like the way things were going. It had been all right before, when just the young one was here. The old one was something else, though. He'd met her type before. They had friends in City Hall; they didn't pay parking tickets and had to be handled with kid gloves. By tomorrow the word would have come down from above to go easy on her.

'Three of the seven immortals,' Polly answered for her niece.

'Come again?'

'They are Chinese jade figures,' she said impatiently. 'They represent the seven immortals. In Chinese mythology, seven men were visited by the gods and given immortality, as well as special gifts — one was given the gift of wisdom, and another the gift of healing. These were three of a set of seven.'

'I take it they're valuable?' he said.

'Priceless.'

He lifted his eyebrows slightly and made a quick mark in his notebook. 'Were they insured?'

'Yes, for fifty thousand each. Of course no amount of money could replace the loss.'

'Of course,' he said, unable to conceal a trace of sarcasm in his voice.

Nancy understood, as he could not,

what her aunt meant. Money did not mean a great deal to Aunt Polly. Someone had once said that there were two classes of people to whom money actually meant very little — those who had always had it, and those who had never had it. Aunt Polly had always had it. But she had been very fond and proud of the three green men. They were the envy of collectors throughout the world and Aunt Polly enjoyed being envied.

'Anything else taken?' the detective asked.

Polly looked in Nancy's direction. 'I don't think so,' Nancy said. 'When I saw the broken case I just called the police, but it doesn't look as if anything else was bothered.'

A uniformed policeman came in from the kitchen. 'Back door's been forced,' he said to the man in charge. The detective made another entry in his notebook.

'What about those other pieces?' he asked of the women, indicating a shelf containing several jade figures. 'Or aren't they valuable?'

'Very,' Polly said.

'Well, if they're so valuable, why weren't they taken too?'

'Presumably because the thief was interested in the three green men,' she said, speaking as one would speak to a stubborn and not very bright child. 'Because those other pieces are only valuable, while to a real collector the three immortals would be virtually priceless. I've been offered many times their appraised worth. The value of art does not necessarily depend upon its price tag, not to the true art lover, at least. Those remaining pieces are expensive, but there are others like them elsewhere. The immortals are unique. They cannot be replaced.'

'You both live here?' the policeman asked.

'The house is mine,' Aunt Polly informed him. 'My niece uses it when she is in the city.'

'Anyone else live here?'

'I have a maid, who is out of town just now.'

He turned his attention back to Nancy. 'Did you get a look at this guy the other time he was here?'

'I didn't see much of his face. He had long hair and a beard and he wore sunglasses. He was tall and strong — not big or hefty, but just strong. And he had reddish hair, and he was a heavy smoker.'

'He was smoking?'

'No, but his fingers were badly stained and there was a strong tobacco smell — he held me rather close. Oh, and there was a long scar, here.' She drew a finger along the back of her hand, up over the wrist. 'A very old one, I'd say.'

He wrote for a moment. 'Are you in San Francisco often?'

'Off and on. I use Aunt Polly's house when I'm here. My aunt raised me as a child. And I have an apartment of my own in Los Angeles.'

'Where were you today?'

She hesitated for a second. She saw the look that flashed across her aunt's face and she suddenly remembered her aunt's suspicions as to why Nancy's father had come to San Francisco.

'I had a luncheon engagement,' Nancy said aloud and looked away from the angry set of Aunt Polly's chin.

The detective seemed not to notice the silent exchange between the two. 'So somebody could have expected you to be out,' he said. She nodded mutely.

'What about you?' he asked of Polly. 'Anybody expect you to be out today?'

'I make no secret of my activities,' she said. 'Neither do I post bulletins. I was shopping. And I had an appointment with my hairdresser. But as he was with me, I suppose he's not suspect.'

'He could have a friend.'

'If you knew my hairdresser, you would never make such a suggestion.'

The man seemed to have exhausted his questions or at least his inclination to ask them. He looked grimly at what he had written, closed the book, and put it in an inside pocket of his coat. Nancy had a glimpse of the gun he wore beneath his coat. The uniformed policemen had apparently finished with their work and were waiting now at the door.

'We'll be in touch,' the detective said, giving each of them a nod. 'I guess you'll be around, won't you?' He aimed that question at Nancy in particular.

'I'm on a leave of absence,' she said. 'I'll be here for several weeks.'

He seemed satisfied with that. He gave them another nod and was gone, taking the officers with him.

When he had gone, Aunt Polly said, 'I wonder, is this the Chinese year of the boar?' She started toward the stairs.

'The lock on the kitchen door was forced,' Nancy said. 'Should we do something about having it replaced before night?'

'That would be locking the barn after the horse is taken. They've already taken all that I care about. By the way, how was the lunch with your father?'

Nancy felt her face redden. 'He didn't show up,' she said, knowing exactly what was in her aunt's mind.

'I thought not.' Aunt Polly disappeared up the stairs.

★　★　★

It was necessary to have a locksmith come to repair the lock on the back door, and by that time Nancy had to begin dressing for her dinner date with Tom.

She was just coming down the stairs when the sound of a key in the front door stopped her. A minute later Ellen came into the hall, setting her bag unceremoniously on the floor.

'Ellen!' Nancy exclaimed. 'I didn't expect you back tonight. How is your sister?'

'As fit as she ever was,' the maid said peevishly. 'Never having been in an accident. It was a trick, a mean cruel joke on somebody's part, sending me off down there all shook up, only to find my sister at home watching TV and wondering what on earth I was doing there, unexpected like.'

'I think I can tell you why it was done,' Nancy said. 'And it was nothing personal against you, I'm sure. Someone just wanted you out of the house. We were robbed this afternoon.'

Ellen's eyes went wide with surprise. 'No! Did they take the green men?'

'That, and nothing else.'

Ellen sighed and shook her head. 'I'll bet herself is fit to be tied.'

'No; as a matter of fact, she's taken it quite calmly.'

'That's what she shows.' Ellen bobbed her head emphatically. 'Just the same, the first thing I'm going to do is make some of that green tea she likes so well and take it up to her.'

Nancy was just thinking that she must tell that policeman — what was his name? Davis, that was it — about the ruse that had been used to get Ellen out of the house, when the phone rang and it was the detective on the line.

'This is a coincidence,' she said when he had identified himself. 'I was just going to call you.'

'I have some questions I want to ask you,' he said. 'I was wondering if it would be possible for you to come by the station.'

Nancy glanced at her watch. Tom was due any minute now. 'It's a little awkward. Couldn't it wait until tomorrow? I'm just going out to dinner.'

'If you'd like, I can come to wherever you're having dinner.' His tone was polite and yet his offer sounded like a threat.

'No, I'll come there,' she said with resignation. 'Give me fifteen minutes.'

She took time enough just to get a coat

and to tell Ellen to explain to Mr. Farroday. She did not bother to get the car from the garage. The station was only a block from the cable car line, which was probably closer than she would be able to park the car. As she travelled toward the station, she was thinking perhaps it was just some such occurrence as this that had prevented her father from meeting her today as planned. She had started several times during the afternoon to call him, but each time hurt pride had stopped her from completing the call. She vowed to call him as soon as she got home.

Detective Davis was not a man to beat around the bush. No sooner had she been ushered into his office and seated at the chair facing his desk than he asked her, 'Why didn't you tell me about your father?'

'I — ' She paused, wondering how much he knew, and if she could get by with a half-truth. 'I . . . didn't think it was important.'

'He was in prison, right?'

She nodded.

'He is now out of prison, and has come

to San Francisco in the last few days, right?'

'He came to see me. We've had no communication for several years.'

'Do you know what he was in prison for?'

'No,' she lied.

'Don't lie to me, Miss Blair — it is Miss Blair, isn't it, and not Miss Dunbar. He was in for armed robbery, and you know that, right?'

'I've been known as a Dunbar since I was a child, but yes, Blair is really correct. And yes, I do know that my father was in prison for armed robbery, although I only learned this the day before yesterday. I had been led to believe that he was dead.'

'Your father, a convicted thief, comes to town. Your aunt, who is wealthy and who he has every reason to resent, is robbed, and you don't think there might be some connection?'

'I'm sure there isn't.'

'Who was your lunch date with this afternoon?'

She felt her pulse quicken. 'My father.'

'And?'

'He didn't show up,' she said reluctantly.

He was silent for a moment. 'The fellow who's travelling with your father says he left with you.'

'That's impossible. I went by the hotel where my father is staying and he wasn't there.'

'What time was that?'

'Eleven — about a minute after when I first arrived there.'

He glanced at some notes on his desk. 'You called to report the robbery at one fifteen. Why did it take you two hours to get back to your house?'

She felt a flush of resentment at being treated like a criminal. 'I drove down to Land's End. I was — I wanted to think.'

'And you didn't just coincidentally see your father there?' he asked smoothly.

'No, I didn't. Perhaps it would save time if you would ask him. I'm sure he'll tell you exactly the same story.'

'We would, if we could find him.'

Something tightened into a ball in her stomach. She gripped the wooden arms of the chair in which she sat, only vaguely aware that she had gotten a splinter in her finger. 'I'm sure he must have come back to his hotel by now,' she said. 'I can give you the name and address of it, if you like.'

'We've already been there. Your father isn't there. His friend says he hasn't been there since he left with you at eleven o'clock this morning.'

Nancy sat speechless for a moment, trying to collect her thoughts into some semblance of order. Finally she asked, 'What are you trying to suggest?'

'I'm not suggesting anything. I'm only gathering facts. Fact, your father is a convicted thief. Fact, he needs money. Fact, your aunt has money. Fact, you arrive in town unexpectedly — you did arrive in town unexpectedly, didn't you?'

'It wasn't exactly unexpected.' She wondered where on earth he had collected his information in such a short time.

'All right, then, sooner than expected, right?' She nodded mutely. 'Your father also arrives in town unexpectedly. You have lunch. You meet again today. He

114

disappears. You come home and call the police to report some jade figures missing. He stays missing.' He paused, staring meaningfully at her.

'And where does the other man fit into your little picture?' she asked sharply.

'Which other man?'

'The one with the beard and the long hair, the one who broke in the other time and attacked me.'

'Oh, yeah, him.' His tone seemed to make an accusation of the reply.

She flushed hotly. 'I didn't make him up. He was there; he nearly strangled me. There were marks on my throat where he . . .'

'They're gone now,' he said quietly.

They were of course gone, faded so that only a really close examination would discover any traces of them. For the first time she began to see how truly incriminating was the evidence the police had marshaled.

'Why didn't you report that other time?'

'My aunt didn't want the bad publicity. And she said it was pointless; that the police wouldn't be interested.'

'The police are always interested, as an aside. Why didn't you report it yourself?'

Why hadn't she? First, because she thought it had been done, and afterward, because her aunt had been so insistent, and because so many other things had been happening to her that she had hardly thought of it. But even as she was collecting these answers in her mind, she saw how thin they would sound expressed like that, removed from the event as it were.

'I don't know,' she said lamely.

He went to a closet and brought a jacket from it. It was a man's sport coat, plaid, cheaply made. He brought it around to where she was sitting and handed it to her.

'Recognize it?'

She fingered the cloth and said honestly, 'No.'

'It's your father's. Notice anything unusual about it?'

Again she shook her head. 'No.'

'Look at the right sleeve.'

She did. 'There's a button missing.'

He held something out to her. She saw that it was a button. It was, almost certainly, the button missing from the jacket, although it was a common enough style of button.

She looked up, directly into the policeman's coolly appraising eyes. 'And where was the button found?' She felt certain she already knew the answer.

'In the kitchen of your aunt's house, just inside the door with the forced lock.'

For a long moment they stared silently at one another. She asked calmly, 'Am I to be arrested?'

He did not answer at once. He took the jacket from her, and the button, and put the one back in the closet, the other into a drawer of his desk. He sat down and again surveyed her. 'I want to see your father,' he said.

She took a deep breath. 'I don't know where he is. And wherever he is, I don't believe that he committed this robbery. Frankly I should like to see him myself; and if I do, I shall try to persuade him to get in touch with you. An innocent man has nothing to fear, has he?'

'That's right.' He stood up. 'You may go, Miss Dunbar.'

She stood also, and said, wishing she didn't sound so defensive, 'Miss Blair. Thank you.'

Outside on the street she discovered that the fog had crept into the city, blurring the outlines of the buildings even across the street. It was cold and damp, weather that just suited her gloomy mood. She stood for a moment, hands thrust deep into her coat. She had an impulse to run, to hide. She, who was innocent, felt the accusing finger pointed at her, and knew for a fact that it was not only the guilty who ran. The fear of false arrest; the shame of accusation; the feeling of inability to cope with something so out of one's elements. These emotions urged her feet to hasten, pleaded with her to disappear into the night and the fog.

She remained motionless on the sidewalk until she had slowed her pounding heart, until the voice of calm had quieted her churning thoughts. At length she walked the block to the cable car stop. It was going on ten, but the streets were still busy with tourists and the city's own night people. The car when it came was full without being packed. She stood at the rear, clinging to the side out of the way of the brakeman who worked the brake lever from this platform.

They began to climb the hill, their ascent seeming at once almost perpendicular. She leaned back, fighting the gravity that wanted to fling her over the railing. The lights of the downtown area sank away beneath her in a spectacular display.

The brakeman went inside to collect fares. She was alone on the platform except for a man who had appeared out of the night and jumped on after her. She had not looked at him, absorbed as she was in her own thoughts.

Now, suddenly, he moved toward her, pressing himself against her. 'Don't move,' he whispered into her ear, 'and don't scream. I've got a knife in your back.'

8

She started and involuntarily turned her head. 'Mick,' she said, recognizing her father's companion almost at once.

Something sharp suddenly pressed against the small of her back and he put an arm about her shoulders to hold her to him. Her eyes went wide, and she felt a weakening in her knees. The car came to a stop. A woman with her arms full of packages got off, pressing past the two of them to descend the steps. Nancy thought how incredible it was that anyone could pass so close and not sense her terror.

'Where is he?' Mick demanded.

'Where is . . . ?' The knife jabbed, making her jerk in his arms.

'Don't lie to me, damn you. He went out to lunch with you and hasn't been back since, and now the police are looking for him. What have you done with him?'

The brakeman was coming back. In a moment he would ask them for their fares. Nancy had made up her mind to scream and throw herself away from Mick's knife. The car would be starting up any second now; she hoped that would throw him sufficiently off balance to enable her to break free of his embrace. She tensed to spring.

Someone a few feet away called, 'Wait.' A young man in a sweater and jeans was running to catch the car.

Mick took her arm in a grip that was painfully firm and moved her toward the steps. 'Come on,' he said.

She looked around over her shoulder, trying to catch the brakeman's eye, but he was looking away. The hand on her arm yanked at her, and she stumbled off the car with him. In a moment the cable car was clanking up the hill.

'Here.' He dragged her toward the shadow of an alleyway running between two closed shops. The fog-thickened darkness swallowed them up. By the time they had gone a few feet into the alley they were enshrouded, invisible to anyone passing by on the street.

He spun her around and flung her against the wall of a building, knocking the breath out of her. Something moved in his hand, and he thrust the knife close enough that she could see it clearly.

'Now, damn you,' he said in a low, menacing voice, 'where is he?'

She did the very last thing she would have wanted to do: she began to cry.

She could not help it. It was not only that she was terrified of him, of the look of madness in his eyes and the switch-blade in his hand. It was the entire chain of events that had brought her to this dark night, this crowded alley. She began to sob quietly, a tear stealing from the corner of her eye to run glistening over her cheek, gathering speed as it went.

Finally he took the knife away and said, 'Stop bawling, for Pete's sake.'

To her surprise, the arm that had been pinning her to the wall pulled her around and she was sobbing against his shoulder while he patted her a bit clumsily, but soothingly nonetheless.

'Don't you really know where he is?' he

asked after a minute.

She managed a gurgled 'No,' and then went back to her crying.

He let her cry until she had cried it all out of her system. Finally the sobs diminished and stopped altogether. He produced a handkerchief from his pocket, crumpled but clean. She dried her eyes and blew her nose quite unceremoniously and looked up at him. He looked not at all menacing now, just very concerned and very unhappy, and tense with strain.

'I'm sorry,' he said, looking all the more miserable. 'I've just been out of my mind, I guess. I've been worrying about the old man — your father, I mean. And when those cops came around — do you know what it will mean if he gets arrested, for anything? Even for jaywalking? They'll throw him back in the pen and toss the key.'

She sniffed again. 'I didn't see him at all today.'

'You went to lunch with him, didn't you?'

She shook her head violently. 'He wasn't there when I came. Nobody was. I came inside and asked for him, and then for you, but both of you were out. I thought I'd been stood up. I thought he just didn't want to see me.' She began to sniff again, threatening another crying spell.

'That's a pretty stupid thing to think,' he said bluntly. 'I mean, he came halfway across the country to get here. You don't think he came to see the Golden Gate Bridge, do you?'

His harsh tone was unflattering, but sobering. 'You're right, of course,' she said. 'I just didn't think. I was so disappointed that he wasn't there.'

'That's the part I don't understand. I told the cops he left with you. I thought he had. He went outside to wait, a little before eleven. I looked out the window once and saw him there. When I looked again he was gone, so I just assumed you had picked him up. I went out myself right after.'

'And I just missed you. You must have come out while I was parking the car.'

He was thoughtful for a moment. When he spoke again, it was in a self-accusatory way. 'I shouldn't have let him go by himself. He's softheaded about things, you know. Like, he's the world's easiest touch. I always like to go out with him when he goes, to keep an eye on him, but I thought this time the two of you would like to be alone. I figured he couldn't get into any trouble with you, in your car. Jeez, if I'd known! He can't even remember to look for the 'walk' and 'don't walk' signs.'

She put a hand on his arm. It was difficult to realize that ten minutes before this man had been threatening her. She could understand the sort of panic that had driven him to such drastic actions, though.

'You mustn't blame yourself.' When he did not reply, she said, 'Would you like a drink somewhere?'

'No, I'd better get back to the hotel. If he was trying to get in touch with me, that's where he'd try. I mean, he may wake up in a hospital or something, maybe like he got hit by a car. I guess I'd better get back there.'

When he looked directly at her again,

he looked truly mortified. 'I must have been crazy. If you were harmed, he'd kill whoever did it.'

'I understand. And I'm not angry.'

Another cable car was just climbing the hill as they came out of the alley. 'I'll see you home,' he said, taking her arm again, but in an entirely different way. She started to protest, but he quickly said, 'I told you, he'd be really broken up if anything happened to you, and it's getting pretty late.'

They said very little on the way. At her stop, he got off with her and walked up the hill until they were outside Aunt Polly's house, dark now. He looked up at it and gave a low whistle.

'I never knew . . . ' he said, and paused. 'I mean, he said rich, but I didn't think . . . ' He left his remarks unfinished.

'If I hear anything, anything at all, I'll get in touch with you,' she promised.

'I'd appreciate it. And about what happened earlier — '

'Forget it. I have.' They exchanged smiles, and then she turned and went up the steps. She unlocked the door and turned to wave to him. He had waited to be sure she got in all right. Now he waved back and started down the hill, hurrying, almost running. She watched until he had disappeared into the fog before she went into the hall, lit only by the night light on the stairs.

Aunt Polly and Ellen had gone to bed. She wondered what had happened to Tom. No doubt he had come, had gotten her message, and gone back to his hotel to wait until he heard from her. She wondered if she ought to call him now, and decided it was probably too late.

She stopped at her aunt's door, listening, but everything seemed still inside, and when she opened the door gently she could distinguish the even breathing that told her Aunt Polly was asleep.

She went along the hall to her own room. It sat at the corner of the house and when the draperies were open at night, as she had left them earlier, the light from the streetlamp on the corner cast a soft glow over the room.

The first thing she saw in the glow were

the feet and legs of the man seated in the big chair against the wall.

In the second in which she paused at the door, he moved out of the chair, standing up and coming toward her.

'Don't scream, for God's sake,' he said in a whisper.

'Tom,' she said, surprised. 'What on earth are you doing here?'

He reached past her to close the door gently. 'Waiting for you. Where's the blasted light switch?'

'Here.' She flicked it on. They stood for a moment blinking at one another, getting used to the light.

'I should have thought you would have had it on before,' she said. 'Or are you accustomed to sitting about in the dark?'

'I didn't want your aunt to discover I was here.'

'May I take it then that Ellen did not show you up here to my room to wait?' she asked, her voice cold. 'I thought it was a little presumptuous of her.'

'Of me, you mean,' he said, grinning. 'No, I broke in as a matter of fact, after they both went to bed.'

'May I ask why? Before you leave, I mean.'

'I wanted to see you. Aren't you happy to see me?'

'Under these circumstances, no.'

'That's a pity. And I was beginning to think something was developing between us.' He took a step closer.

'Don't touch me,' she said, backing against the door.

He laughed, which only infuriated her. 'Relax. I'm not going to fling you to the floor and assault you. I just wanted to be sure that door was shut.'

'I'm not sure I wouldn't rather it was open.'

'Oh, come off it. I'll admit it was a little brash of me to climb in a window and wait for you in the dark like this.'

'A little brash?'

'But let's face it, if I were going to attack you, I'd have started right off, without all this conversation. And anyway, I've had better chances, wouldn't you say?'

She sighed and went past him to put her purse on the dresser. 'I ask myself, what sort of a man would break into a woman's house and scare her half to death?' She hung up her coat and seated herself primly on the chair. There was only the one chair, and for obvious reasons she had decided not to seat herself on the bed. 'And now,' she said, 'I'd like to know what this is about.'

'Ellen told me you had gone to the police station. They wanted to question you about something.'

'That's right,' she said guardedly.

'What about?'

'I'm not sure I want to tell you.'

'Okay, then I'll tell you. They think you and your father arranged this entire robbery between you. He's missing and they found a button of his here, in the kitchen. They think that previous break-in was just a cover-up story you invented. Am I doing all right so far?'

She looked at him wide-eyed. 'Very. But how do you know all this?'

'Because they talked to me earlier.'

'But why you? What has any of this to do with you?'

'I wish I knew some nice way to explain, without making you angry, but I guess I may as well get this over with. You'd better have a look at this.' He took a wallet from his pocket and handed it across to her. It was opened to an identification card. She read it and her mouth fell open.

'You're a detective,' she said, looking up at him again.

'An insurance investigator.'

'But why . . . oh.' She put a hand to her mouth and frowned. 'That's why you were so interested in meeting me. And I thought . . . '

'That was the original reason. Look, there's no way to keep from sounding like a heel, so I'll just plow into it, and later maybe we can pick up the pieces, all right? My company held the policy on a jade figurine that was stolen.'

'Three of them, you mean.'

He shook his head. 'No, the one before that, in Boston.'

'In Boston?' She looked more than a little bewildered.

'You didn't know?'

'Know what? I'm afraid I'm very confused.'

'I would have thought . . . Well, that needs some more explaining. One of our policy-holders in Boston owned one of those blasted figurines and it got stolen. It was a bit suspicious because, as in your aunt's case, nothing but the jade piece was stolen. When we did a little investigating, we found that still another one had been stolen a few months ago back in Chicago. It didn't get much coverage, but the second one coming up missing made the newspapers. I would have thought even the papers out here would have carried some mention of it.'

'They may have, if it was recent. I wasn't reading the newspapers.'

He lifted one eyebrow. 'That man you were going with?'

'What? Oh, him. Yes.' She avoided his gaze.

'Were you in love with him?'

'No,' she said, not seeming to mind that his question was entirely personal and hardly pertinent to an investigation of robbery. 'I wanted to be — I even tried to be — but I suppose he realized our relationship wasn't going anywhere.'

'Anyway,' he said, going back to his narrative, 'the disappearance of two of the seven figures led us to believe someone was out to collect the set, so I went out on the trail, so to speak. One of them is owned by a man in Seattle, another by a woman here in San Francisco, and of course three of them belong to your aunt.'

'Belonged,' she corrected him.

'Well, yes. And that brought me to you, first as a routine matter. Your appearance in San Francisco when you weren't expected was a question mark that I had to check out. And then when I followed you here, and just after you came in, a man came out who looked like the suspect that had been described to us — someone got a glimpse of the man in Boston. Well, I had to check you out a little more closely.'

She gave him a rueful smile. 'And I thought it was all my famous charm.'

'That's the worst of it. I know there's no way to make this sound convincing, but after we'd met, all the interest I was showing in you . . . that was genuine.'

She stood up, brushing some imaginary dust from her skirt front. 'You needn't soften me up with sweet words. I'll cooperate as far as I can.'

He came to her in one quick step, and before she could object or move away, he took her in his arms and kissed her hotly, demandingly. At first she struggled against him and then, because her heart wasn't in the struggle, she gave it up.

It seemed forever before he released her. When he did, his breath was short and his voice sounded foreign. 'Don't say that sort of thing again, ever,' he said.

It was not for a moment more that something he had said came back to her and she exclaimed, 'But Tom, if you saw that man, you could tell the police he was real.'

'I already did.'

'But that detective said . . . '

'He was bluffing. Trying to scare you. What he wants is your father. They believe he's their thief.'

'I don't believe that. He can't be. For one thing, there's that other man.'

'Who could be a hired man,' Tom

134

pointed out gently.

'For another, how could my father afford that sort of travelling around — Boston, Chicago, San Francisco?'

'If he had been hired by somebody also, some collector who wanted the set, they would no doubt have given him a fee in advance.'

She brushed a hand wearily over her brow. 'I just can't accept that. If you had seen him ... And Mick would have known, I'm sure, and he didn't. I saw him. He's as bewildered as I.'

Tom sighed. 'If your father had nothing to do with this, why did he just disappear like that? Where is he?'

She met his gaze frankly, and he saw fear glimmering in her eyes. 'I wish I knew,' she said.

9

At that moment, Harvey Blair was seated in a wooden chair in a shabby room not more than a fifteen-minute drive from Nancy's own room. He was bound hand and foot to the chair, and gagged. He had been tied like this since late morning, since he had been tricked out of his meeting with Nancy. His initial reaction had been one of rage that anyone should tie him up like this. The ropes were cruelly tied and gnawed at his wrists and ankles, and the gag was sheer horror. Something had been shoved into his mouth, threatening to strangle him, and another cloth was bound tightly around the lower half of his face. The cloth pressed on his tongue, drying his mouth painfully.

Earlier he had been struck on the head, and his head still throbbed with the pain of that blow. He wanted to put his hand up to feel the wound, only of course he could not lift his hands.

He was not alone just now, although he had been off and on throughout the afternoon and night. He had come out of the dark unconsciousness to find himself tied in the chair and confronted with a wild-eyed man with a beard and long hair.

At first he had thought the man in the room with him was merely crazy. Throughout the long afternoon and evening, and now into the night, he had watched with anxious eyes: watched his captor go out and come in, out and in; watched and listened as the man talked on the telephone. Now the bearded man waited, waited for a special delivery to be made.

At least, he knew the name of his captor's particular brand of insanity. It was called smack. Heroin. The man was as much a prisoner as Harvey Blair himself was, bound to a habit that ruled his every moment. The bearded man was an addict and, from all indications, pretty heavily into the stuff. Harvey Blair had seen this often enough before, in prison, to recognize the symptoms when he saw them.

The bearded man's contact was late. For ten minutes the man had been pacing up and down in the room, up and down, scratching and muttering as he walked. Alternately he took a hunting knife from atop the plastic-covered kitchen table and cleaned his fingernails with it. Several times he faced the man tied in the chair and brandished the knife threateningly.

'You,' he said, his voice rasping. 'You I'm going to kill. You and that snotty girl.' He bobbed his head up and down for emphasis. 'Oh yeah. Certain people don't know that. Certain people think this is all some kind of game. They think when this is done I'm going to clear out and leave you and that girl to point fingers at me later. But I'm not stupid. Oh no. When I clear out, there won't be any witnesses left. I made the mistake of letting that girl live once, because she caught me by surprise and I wasn't thinking as clearly as I should have been. But I'll make up for that.'

Harvey Blair, his mouth filled with

dirty cloth, could only stare into the wild abyss of the man's eyes. He had lived most of his adult life in prison, among murderers and thieves and criminals of every conceivable sort. He had always counseled himself that so long as a threat came from a man, a man with however limited a mind, there was always the possibility of coping with that mind, and the man.

But a junkie wasn't a man anymore; he was an animal. He was all the savage elements of man's bestial nature, held in check by one fragile thread. That fragile thread was his fix, and if that thread went . . .

The bearded man took a step toward him. The hand that held the knife was shaking as if he were palsied.

Someone knocked at the door.

★   ★   ★

'Well, I thought perhaps the police had sent you straight off to prison,' Aunt Polly greeted her niece in the morning. 'What on earth did those people want this time?'

Nancy seated herself rather dispiritedly and helped herself to a cup of coffee. 'They wanted to ask some further questions.'

Aunt Polly was not so easily put off as that. 'Such as?'

'He wanted to ask about my father. He had somehow learned about him and his prison record.'

'There's nothing mysterious about that. I told him.'

'You? Why on earth would you do that?'

'Because I thought it was germane. And you needn't look so aghast. You knew what I thought about him from the beginning. As soon as the jade figures were taken, I suspected him.'

Nancy was about to say something more, but she was simply not up to trying to play peacemaker between her father and her aunt, not at this particular moment.

'I don't suppose he's been found,' Aunt Polly asked.

'No.'

Later, when Nancy was preparing to

leave the breakfast room, Polly said, 'By the way, we've been invited to the Chengs' this evening for dinner and a moon festival party.'

'I'm not sure . . . ' Nancy started to say, but her aunt did not let her finish.

'I told them you might have a date, as you'd been seeing someone, and they insisted that you bring your gentleman along.'

As he was leaving the previous night, Tom had asked to meet Aunt Polly and Nancy herself had thought several times about introducing them. This would be an ideal opportunity for them to get acquainted in a relaxed, sociable atmosphere. And although she did not exactly feel like celebrating, she could see that a moon festival might be just the very thing she needed to take her out of herself.

'Very well,' she said aloud. 'I'll be seeing Tom for lunch. I'll see if he's free.'

She had been awake far into the night, long after she had helped Tom steal from the house, thinking of him and reliving the entire scene that had just been played between them. He had left with a repeated warning that if her father was involved in the jade robberies, as the police believed, she herself might be in danger.

Despite her concern for her father, it was not this conversation between her and Tom that most lingered in her mind. Again and again her thoughts went back to the moment when Tom had kissed her.

If only the truth about his profession had not marred their relationship. How could she believe that his interest in her was genuine when it was also a part of his job?

As things stood, he represented a threat to her father. She had made up her mind that, if she found her father before Tom or the police did, she would inform only Mick, and somehow she would help her father to escape the city and hide himself in some distant place. She had no great wealth herself, but in addition to the salary she earned from the airlines, her aunt gave her an allowance. She had in fact more than she needed, and had been able to build up a modest bank account.

If she had to, she could secretly provide

for her father, for years if need be, with no grave hardship to herself. She had enough cash that she could help him get out of the country, even, perhaps to Mexico or South America, someplace where he could live reasonably. She did not care that her actions might be looked upon as illegal. She was convinced of her father's innocence.

She knew, though, that such a course of action would forever place a barrier between her and Tom. She could never come to him in the openness of a really meaningful relationship. Without honesty, love could not exist.

Very simply, her choice was between Tom or her father. For twenty years her father had been punished for love, and had been denied the company of wife or daughter or, with one exception, friends. He had earned a right to first place in her consideration.

She hadn't the slightest idea, however, how to go about finding him.

★   ★   ★

'And what is a moon festival party?' Tom asked.

They were at Union Square. They passed a flower vendor's kiosk and Nancy slowed her steps slightly, giving her attention momentarily to the display of blossoms.

'I'll have one of those,' she said, pointing to some yellow sweethearts.

She carried it as they moved with the foot traffic. 'The moon festival is the second most important of the Chinese festivals, just behind the Chinese New Year. It's more or less a harvest festival, but more to toast next year's crops and food supply and to wish success in upcoming ventures. Traditionally the party will be held outside, for moon-viewing.'

'I think I remember something about it. Isn't everyone supposed to pay off their debts and settle all the family quarrels?'

'No — that's New Year's.'

They emerged on the opposite side of the square, and moved with noontime shoppers and throngs of office workers on their lunch breaks, across the street. On the other side they detached themselves from the larger stream of walkers to make their way toward a cable car stop. One of the antiquated cars was just climbing the hill, its bells clanging. In a moment they had climbed aboard and were swaying and bouncing their way up the hill. Younger riders stood on the side steps, heeding the brakeman's warnings to lean in when they passed another car going downhill, close enough that the outside riders on the two cars could easily have touched if they tried.

In Chinatown they stopped at one of the many shops. Nancy held up a round lantern for Tom's notice. 'At a moon festival you give paper lanterns,' she explained. 'The shapes are symbolic. These, of course, are moon-shaped, and rather standard.' She put it aside and held up one in a butterfly shape. 'This would be given for longevity. And that one shaped like a carp might be given to a scholar, for success through endeavor.'

She bought a selection of the paper lanterns, to take along that evening as gifts and they moved on to their next stop, a Chinese bakery. 'The one essential gift,' she explained as she made her purchase, 'is a box of four moon cakes.'

The moon cakes were small cakes with Chinese figures imprinted on top. They looked somewhat like American breakfast rolls, but as she explained to him, were heavy like American fruitcakes.

'They're baked of moon flour, or gray flour, and spices and almonds and fruits and nuts, and plenty of sugar. Aside from the fact that they are delicious, the Chinese have a traditional reason for eating the moon cakes. In the fourteenth century China was ruled by the brutal Mongols who kept the Chinese nobles in Peking literally under their thumbs. The Mongols planted spies everywhere, even among the household servants, so that the Chinese nobles dared not complain or make plans against their tyrants, not even in the privacy of their own homes.

'The Mongols were afraid, and rightly so, that the nobles hoped eventually to form a rebellion. The Chinese women-folk, however, devised their own system of secret communication. With the approach of the moon festival, the ladies baked messages hidden in their moon cakes. The special cakes were sent as presents to the homes of all the people who could be counted on to take part in an uprising. Every would-be rebel was told where to be and the exact time to strike.

'The plot was successful. Armed with cleavers and clubs and every sort of makeshift weapon, the rebels overthrew the surprised garrison in Peking and started the war that eventually drove the tyrants from the whole country.'

Tom bit into a cake and held the exposed side up to examine it. 'Well, no messages hidden here. It looks like there's no uprising planned for tonight.'

'And yet,' she said a little sadly, 'these people aren't much freer than those others were.' She gestured at the street outside the shop window. 'This is perhaps the least understood or publicized of all the ghettos. The isolation that has allowed these people to preserve many of their traditions has also allowed most of them to remain virtually enslaved. Many of them work for starvation wages for the powerful tongs. Many are people who came into the country illegally and thus dare not go to the police, regardless of how they are debased or used. Inside Chinatown they are bound with virtually unbreakable chains to a past that insists upon treating women as slaves and men as expendable, while outside the community they face horrible prejudice and ignorance.'

'And in the homeland, millions of them are slaves to new tyrants,' he said. 'Yes, it's true, probably no people in history have been so exploited as the Chinese, both here and in their own country. And when you think of how the average Caucasian thinks of the Oriental — mysterious, evil men running dens of iniquity.'

'Well, you for one will see tonight how entirely erroneous that concept is. I'll see you at five?'

'Don't you want me to take you home now?'

'No. I have some other errands to run and you aren't here just to see the sights.'

'No one's going to question how I do my business.'

'Nevertheless,' she said, 'I would much prefer that you spend some of your time trying to find my father, if you can.'

'And if I do find him? What then?'

She could not help wondering if he knew what her thoughts were along those lines. She avoided his direct gaze and said, 'I would very much appreciate it if you would bring him to me before — before anybody else.'

'You know, it would be futile and foolish of you to try to help him escape from the police. If he is innocent, it will be far better for him to cooperate openly and help clear his name.'

'Only no one will be trying to do that, will they? Haven't the police already made up their minds as to his guilt?'

'Maybe the police have, but I haven't. Trust me, please.'

She did look up at him then. 'Trust is something that must be earned.' She did not wait for a reply, but turned from him and moved away into the crowds of shoppers.

She had not explained to Tom, but her other 'errand' was a visit to her father's hotel. She felt certain that he had not yet returned there, or she would have heard from one source or another, but there was always the possibility, however slim, that Mick might have some news to pass on to her. Even if he did not, there was a certain comfort in visiting briefly with someone who felt, at least in this one respect, as she did.

It was not a long trip to the hotel, which was in one of the city's less savory neighborhoods. At one time the area had been the center of activities for the so-called flower children, the beginnings of the hippie movement. Then the atmosphere of loving affection had been an almost palpable presence. Young men with beards and young women with waist-length hair had spoken with gentle voices and handed flowers to passing strangers.

The drug scene, like a bird of prey swooping down on unsuspecting victims, had descended, and the dream neighborhood had become a nightmare. The 'flower children' with their gentle voices and their open affection had become hardened addicts, with sharp eyes searching for potential sources of cash with which to supply their habits. Crime had become a way of life, and love was only another means of earning money.

Nancy took a taxi because her packages were awkward for a bus, and there were no cable cars in this part of town. She got off at the hotel and went in.

'I'm sorry,' the man at the desk told her, eyeing her in an appraising way, 'the gentleman is out. Was he expecting you?'

'No,' she said, and then asked, 'You don't know where he might have gone, do you?'

'Sometimes in the afternoons he goes to Golden Gate Park.'

It was not a very helpful suggestion; the park was immense. She could wander for hours and never see Mick there.

Her disappointment must have shown on her face because the man across the reception desk added, 'I believe he likes to go up by the lake.'

'Thank you,' she said, smiling. 'I'll see if I can find him there. Would you mind if I left my packages here?'

'Sure thing. I'll just put them back here.'

Freed from her packages, it was easy to

catch a bus that took her into the park. Golden Gate Park was the original site of the turn-of-the-century exposition that had been held in the city. Many of the park's attractions were left over from that time — windmills, Japanese tea-houses, and band shells still used for Sunday concerts. There were other significant displays too — at one point what appeared to be the portals of a very fine old house stood by themselves against a backdrop of greenery. They were exactly what they seemed: all that had been left of one of the fine old mansions destroyed by the great earthquake and fire, and placed in the park as a reminder to succeeding generations of the havoc that had been wreaked.

Although it was in the heart of the city, the man-made lake had an idyllic charm that appeared authentic. The lake curved about and was ringed by shrubs and trees among which wandered country-like paths. On the water small electric boats and others powered by foot pedals skimmed the surface at leisurely speeds, hardly disturbing the ducks that swam near the edge and begged food from strolling tourists.

Luck was with her, however, as she had only walked a short distance before she saw Mick walking in her direction. He looked up and recognized her.

'Miss Blair,' he said, looking genuinely pleased to see her and a trifle expectant as well.

'Have you heard anything?' they both began at once, and then paused and laughed, with a note of disappointment in both voices.

He took her arm lightly. 'I guess we were both hoping for some sort of miracle. Just out strolling?'

'I was looking for you, on the outside chance you might have heard something.' She fell into step with him. 'The man at your hotel said I might find you here.'

'It's where I come to escape from things.' He glanced around. 'All this greenery and openness. When I was in prison I used to dream of a spot like this and wonder what it would be like to be free again, to wander along a path beside the water, to see people passing by with happy faces, some of them laughing.'

'I hope the reality is as nice as your dreams.'

'It is, and it isn't. I've learned we're never any freer than our thoughts let us be. Like now — technically I'm free, but I'm tied to the city, tied to a mystery. If I were absolutely free, I'd be free of my friendship with your Dad, for instance. That's a tie too. But I wouldn't want that.'

They had come to a landing pier where people could rent the boats they had seen on the lake. On an impulse, she said, 'Let's rent a boat.'

He grinned in little-boy fashion and said, 'Great.' In a few minutes they had paid a tow-headed young man for the rental of one of the electric boats and were moving slowly out into the lake.

They did not speak for several minutes, each lost in their own thoughts. 'What will you do when my father shows up?' Nancy asked finally.

'That depends.'

He avoided her gaze when she turned to him. 'I suppose you mean it depends on whether he is still under suspicion of robbery.'

He nodded.

'I've been thinking of that myself,' she said. 'I had it in mind that if we could locate him before the police — assuming that for some reason unknown to us he is hiding from the police and not still missing for some other reason — I thought perhaps I could give the two of you some money to go away somewhere. Out of the country, I mean.'

He gave her a surprised look. 'You'd do that?'

'He is my father.'

He nodded and for a moment stared down into the water gliding past the side of the boat. He dropped his hand over the side and trailed his fingers in the water.

'It's up to him, whether he'd want to take any money,' he said. 'We can always manage, get by, you know. The thing is to find him.'

'Haven't you any idea where he might be, if he were hiding?'

'No. But I don't believe he's in hiding. If he were, he would have found some way to contact me by now.'

'And he hasn't.'

'No. So to my mind that means wherever he is, he can't get in touch for one reason or another. Maybe he's in a hospital, or maybe he's already in jail somewhere and the police aren't telling us because they think . . . ' He paused and shrugged. 'Who knows why?'

She looked around, trying to will her thoughts into some sort of order. Suddenly she gasped and instinctively put a hand on Mick's.

'What is it?'

They had been moving slowly about a bend in the channel provided for the boats, past a curtain of trees and shrubbery that all but hid the path at several points. She looked back the way they had come, but she could see nothing but greenery now.

A moment before, she had thought she saw a familiar face — a man standing at one of the trees, looking through the leaves in their direction. She had had only a glimpse of him, but she thought it was the bearded man who had attacked her in Aunt Polly's house.

10

'I thought I saw someone,' she said, looking right and left to see where he might have disappeared to. 'Oh, Mick, if only we could find him.'

'Who?'

'The burglar — the man who really stole the jade figurines.'

'And you saw him? You know who he is?'

'Yes. Oh, there isn't time to explain that now. Can we park this thing and get out for a minute?'

He looked toward the bank where a sign forbade landing the boats. He ignored that and turned in toward the grassy bank. 'Sure we can.'

He jumped into the shallow water and pulled the little boat ashore, dragging it far enough up onto the grass that it would not drift back out into the water.

'This way,' she said, hurrying back the way they had come.

She reached the place where the man had been standing, but there was no one there just now, only a still-smoldering cigarette where someone had tossed it on the ground.

'What's he look like?' Mick asked, looking around. The roadway was only a few feet away here, and cars were going by at regular intervals.

'He has long hair, reddish brown, and a beard and sunglasses.'

Mick pointed. 'Is that him?'

She followed his gesture. 'It — it could be. I can't tell from this distance.'

'Come on,' he said, taking her arm. They began to run along the path, circling some startled-looking tourists who had been trying to photograph the ducks in the water. Ahead, a man in patched jeans disappeared down a path. They reached the point where he had vanished into the trees, down another path that led to the main roadway through the park.

For a moment their quarry seemed to have vanished. Then Nancy saw him down the road a distance, just climbing into a parked Volkswagen.

'There,' she said, but the car pulled out into the traffic and was gone.

They stopped and stood there for a moment looking after the fading tail-lights, feeling defeated. 'It may not have been the same man,' Nancy said, trying to dispel the cloud of gloom that had descended.

'But if it was . . . ' he said, clenching and unclenching his fists.

After a moment she gave a gentle tug at his sleeve. 'We'd better go back and straighten up about that boat, before we have the police looking for us too.'

They went slowly back up the path to the lake. As they walked, he said, 'What I don't understand is, if it was the man you thought it was, what was he doing here, following you?'

'I don't know. If it was him, it may only have been coincidence that he showed up here. Or maybe he was following me.'

'But why?'

She glanced up at him, and he saw, behind the calm poise that she ordinarily displayed, the glint of fear in her eyes. It occurred to him, as it had to her, that if the man who had stolen the figurines was following her, it could only represent a threat. If that man was the thief, and was following Nancy, it was almost certainly because he meant to eliminate her as a witness.

★   ★   ★

They took a taxi back to his hotel and Nancy retrieved her packages. They had been silent since they had left Golden Gate Park. She had been preoccupied and he had been unable to offer anything in the way of genuine encouragement. He knew what it was like to live in the shadow of danger; inside prison walls, danger was never more than a footstep away. Each sound behind you could mean death, each shadow moving in the night a threat to your safety or your life.

The ways he had learned to adjust to and cope with that presence were not ways, however, that he could impart to this slim, fragile-looking girl with him. He did not even want to tell her, 'Always look to see who's behind you.' She already looked like she was scared of her shadow and he was afraid that warning, almost second nature to him, would only serve to scare her more.

'Good luck, and be careful,' was all that he could muster.

'Stay in touch,' she said, attempting — but failing — to look unconcerned, and then was gone in the waiting cab. Mick stood at the plate-glass windows of the lobby and watched until the cab had disappeared into the stream of traffic in the street. Out of habit he glanced back over his shoulder before he turned around, but there was no one there but the desk clerk, who had been watching them with a knowing smirk on his face.

'Pretty girl,' he said as Mick crossed the small and shabby lobby.

Irritated at the suggestion in the man's look, Mick did not bother to reply, but went wordlessly past him to the stairs, with their worn carpeting, that led upstairs to his room on the second floor — the room with the dirty mattress and the glaring light hanging from the center of the ceiling, and the peeling wallpaper that exposed yellowed plaster underneath.

Like a homing device, his thoughts, touching upon all those things, came back to the one question that had been running over and over through his mind: Where was Harvey?

*   *   *

It was already late in the afternoon by the time Nancy arrived back at the mansion in Pacific Heights. Aunt Polly was dressed for dinner by this time and looked a little impatiently at her niece as she came in, her arms laden with her packages.

'I was beginning to think you'd forgotten the Chengs' party,' she said.

'It'll only take me minutes to dress. Mr. Farroday is joining us, by the way. He'll be here at five.'

'I'm not surprised,' Aunt Polly said drily.

*   *   *

With time limited, Nancy brushed her hair energetically until it gleamed, and pulled it back tightly from her face, fastening it with a silver clip. She had chosen a silvery gray silk sheath dress with a mandarin collar, and with it she wore midnight-blue accessories. The gray and blue seemed to suit the night. The dress shimmered in the light as she moved, as if she, too, reflected the moon's pale glory on this special night of the moon.

Ellen was just opening the door to Tom as Nancy came down the stairs. She paused halfway down. He looked up and saw her, and his eyes gleamed with appreciation. 'The moon is going to be jealous,' he said.

She came down the rest of the way, into his arms. He kissed her lightly. From within the living room, Aunt Polly cleared her throat emphatically. Nancy brought Tom in to introduce him to her. 'I've been wanting to meet you,' he said.

'You seem to make a career of wanting to meet us,' she replied. She did not wait for a reply to that remark, but said, 'I thought we would take the Bentley. Will you drive, Mr. Farroday?'

The streets were still crowded with the after-work crush. 'Dinner is early,' Aunt Polly explained as they moved slowly through the streets, 'so that we can retire to the garden outside and enjoy the moon. The Chengs have an honored guest with them, Doctor Li from Taiwan. I believe he's here to lecture on Chinese literature at the university.'

'The weather is perfect,' Nancy said. She turned to Tom. 'The behavior of the elements is another omen for the crops and the food supply for next year.'

'You'll see some very valuable pieces tonight,' Aunt Polly said. 'It's a tradition that those who have curios put them on display for the evening. Oftentimes one sees priceless relics that are otherwise stored in vaults.'

'Isn't that dangerous?' he said. 'I would think it would encourage theft.'

'The custom is little known except among the Chinese themselves, and by the time they've gotten through the usual complement of wine served at a moon festival, none of them would be able to steal anything. I'm usually fortunate if I can walk upright.'

He thought perhaps this was meant to be funny, but he noted that no smile softened the stark lines of her face. Not sure what he should do, he concentrated on driving the Bentley.

There were ten in all for dinner — the traditional number for seating at one table, as Aunt Polly explained. Besides the hosts, Mr. and Mrs. Cheng, there were the guests of honor, Mr. and Mrs. Li and their son, who was somewhere near Nancy's age, and another local couple whom Nancy had met at another such party.

The Chengs greeted them in the living room; Tom could see a dining room through an open doorway, the table already set. A manservant brought them cups of tea served in porcelain as thin as an eggshell. Tom tried to identify the tea, but it was something delicious and unknown to him.

They were introduced to the guests of honor and to the others. It was the first visit for the Lis to the United States, and while the young Mr. Li affected nonchalance, his parents were quite simply delighted. 'All this television,' Mrs. Li said. 'I don't know how American wives get anything done, with all that television to watch.'

'That question often comes up among American husbands,' Aunt Polly said drily.

Mrs. Cheng had gone from the room to attend to some last-minute preparations. Now she came in again and whispered to her husband, who turned to the guests of honor and said, 'Well, shall we have dinner?'

To Tom's surprise, although Mr. Cheng had spoken plainly, the Lis stood as if they hadn't heard him. No one made a move toward the dining room. Again Mr. Cheng addressed the Lis, this time more insistently. 'Shall we eat?' he asked.

This time the visitors got the message. They bowed to him and went toward the dining room, only to stop before the door as if they had suddenly gone shy. Mr. Li implored the others to enter the dining room before them.

By this time Tom had recognized their reluctance for what it was, the Chinese manners of humility. Finally, when their protests at being honored were appropriately registered, the Lis surrendered and led the way into the dining room, followed by the others.

There was more bashful protest over the places at the table, but at last everyone was seated: the Chengs with their backs to the kitchen so that they would get most of the noise from that room, and the Lis opposite them. The cold dishes were already waiting in the center of the table; the food had been arranged Chinese fashion in elaborate patterns of blended or contrasting colors.

'I apologize for the poor meal we are about to serve you,' Mr. Cheng said. Mrs. Cheng, far from protesting at this criticism of her skills, smiled in agreement.

Doctor Li said, 'You must not be modest. The whole world knows your hospitality, which is of the very best.'

A manservant had filled the little wine cups. Mr. Cheng toasted Doctor Li, and the two men drained their cups. When they had been refilled, Mr. Cheng raised his again to toast the entire company, who toasted him back.

Mr. Cheng gestured with his chopsticks toward the cold dishes. 'Please don't be shy,' he said. 'Serve yourselves.' And the meal began.

Nancy had given Tom some idea of what to expect, but even so, the traditional and mistaken idea of light Chinese meals had left him not quite prepared for the sumptuous banquet they were presented with.

As they ate, the guests regularly toasted one another, while the manservant kept their wine cups refilled. Mr. Li raised his cup to Tom and said, 'Kan Pei!'

He looked quizzically at Nancy, and she translated for him: 'Bottoms up.' Grinning, Tom emptied his cup and, following Mr. Li's example, turned it upside down to show that he was not cheating and had emptied it.

The next course was lobster in a spicy sauce. After that, the servant came to remove the plates, and Tom, who was beginning to feel stuffed, thought the dinner was finished; but the plates were at once replaced with clean ones, the guests were given hot steamed towels to wipe their faces and hands, and the banquet went on.

Tom found he was barely able to taste the dessert, and it was with a sense of relief that he finally rose from the table with the others.

'Now what?' he asked Nancy as they re-entered the living room.

'Now,' she said in a whisper, 'we will go out to the garden and contemplate the moon, and the men will recite poetry. I rather suspect that Doctor Li will do the main honors, since that's his specialty.'

At Mr. Cheng's suggestion, they retired to a small walled patio beyond the living room. It was night by now and the moon was in her full splendor overhead. San Francisco nights were often cool but the walls of the garden sheltered them from the ocean breezes, and a hibachi provided just the right amount of warmth.

Although everyone was quite stuffed by the dinner, there was a mood of gaiety. More wine was served, warmed to ward off any evening chills. There was more laughter and joking, and presents were

169

exchanged — the traditional paper lanterns, and the moon cakes. Mrs. Cheng piled the moon cakes on a table in a pyramid.

When Tom found his wine cup being filled yet again, he said, 'How do you tell whether the glow is from the moon or from the wine?'

'Ah well,' said Doctor Li, 'drinking and poetry are hand-in-hand in the Chinese tradition. The Chinese poets, especially the immortal Li Po, were great drinkers. It is said they tried to make up for the puritanism of the traditional Chinese life.'

There was a murmur of appreciation from the guests, who had taken seats in a semicircle about the learned professor. All other conversation had ceased, and it seemed perfectly natural that Doctor Li should begin to lecture them upon the Chinese poets.

'One must feel Chinese poetry, rather than judge it,' he said, speaking especially to the Occidentals present, who could be expected to have the most difficulties with understanding the poetry.

'It is unfortunate that you can have it

only in translation, for certain subtleties are hidden. You do not see the picturesque written characters, each a monosyllable and yet each expressing an idea. You do not see the lines, from top to bottom and from right to left, in the Chinese fashion, or the meter and rhyme in the ancient style, nor the tones, flats and sharps, which give the poems their special beat. A Chinese poem in its original form is as precious and as polished as the Hawthorne vase of Mrs. Cheng that we all so admired in her dining room.'

He bowed in Mrs. Cheng's direction, and each of the guests took time to acknowledge the loveliness of the Hawthorne vase. Then he resumed his lecture on the life and work of Li-Po, the 'Keats of China.'

Later, on the way home, Nancy leaned sleepily against Tom's shoulder and thought of one of the bittersweet poems that Doctor Li had recited. It had reminded her of her father and his years of confinement. How at last he had been set free, to seek her out.

What had happened to him since? Was he once again held somewhere a prisoner, longing for family and friends? Would he spend all of his life apart from the places he wanted to be, the people he wanted to see?

Her eyes misted with tears, and she made a vow to herself that somehow she would find her father again. Perhaps it was too late to give him the daughter he had lost, but at least she could give him freedom, and perhaps some peace of mind.

She glanced up at the silvery moon, and promised that she would find him.

11

When she rose in the morning, Nancy knew what she was going to do.

All but two of the owners of the jade figurines had been robbed. Of the seven figurines, five were now in the hands of the thief, whoever he was. One of the remaining pair was in Seattle, unless it too had recently been stolen. The seventh was here in San Francisco and belonged to a woman named Leach.

She had decided to pay a visit to Mrs. Leach. She did not know exactly what she hoped to accomplish, not having thought things through that far ahead, but whoever was stealing the jade pieces was certainly after the set and Mrs. Leach had one of the few missing pieces to the set. If they did no more than compare notes, something might present itself to them.

She knew who Mrs. Leach was, and where she lived, by virtue of the fact that Aunt Polly had often talked of the woman. On several occasions her aunt had tried without success to persuade the other woman to sell her the fourth green man.

'I can't think what good one will do her,' Aunt Polly had said on more than one occasion. Mrs. Leach, however, had politely but firmly refused to part with the jade figurine that she owned.

Nancy did not mention her plans to her aunt or to Tom. It was no more than a few blocks to where Mrs. Leach lived, in another of the city's fading but still picturesque older houses, and she went before lunch.

A young-looking woman in a maid's uniform opened the door just a crack and peered out cautiously. Nancy gave her name, and added that she was Polly Dunbar's niece. 'Wait there,' the woman said, and closed the door before Nancy could object to being left standing on the front steps.

The maid was back in a very few minutes however, and this time she was pleasant and chatty; apparently Nancy had been given a clean bill of health.

'We read in the papers that you was robbed,' the maid said as she led the way up the broad stairs. 'I've been scared to death we was next. I'm half-afraid to open the door.'

'It's probably just as well to be careful,' Nancy said.

'The missus has been taken to bed. All this excitement. This is her room here.'

Mrs. Leach was not exactly in bed, but rather upon a pale yellow chaise longue heaped with pillows in Japanese silk. She looked more as if she were holding an audience than convalescing. She also looked unabashedly comfortable in a loose wrapper of nebulous style. On the small table beside her was a box of chocolates, from which she was just taking one as Nancy came in.

She popped the chocolate into her mouth and said around it, 'Hello. Have some candy?'

'Thank you, no,' Nancy said.

Mrs. Leach licked a finger clean and eyed Nancy. 'So you're Polly Dunbar's girl,' she said. 'She talked about you a lot whenever I saw her.'

Nancy was surprised, but she said, 'I'm actually only her niece. My own mother died when I was a child.'

'And your father went to jail. Oh, you needn't get excited; there's very little about the people in San Francisco that I don't know, but I keep things to myself. In the first place, most of the so-called society people here wouldn't mingle with me anyway; we were considered nouveau riche. And as far as any shame being attached to your background, my father was in and out of the pokey more times than I can count, although my dear departed husband would have been mortified to hear me tell anyone that.'

Nancy hardly knew how to answer such remarks, and could only murmur, 'Your maid tells me you haven't been well.'

Mrs. Leach gave a flick of her hand. 'I'm not allowed to trouble myself about things anymore. My heart's a bit fluttery. Doctor says I'm to do just as I please and worry about nothing. He's a wonderful doctor; it took me years to find one that I was compatible with. Now I can read those naughty novels, and eat lots of chocolate and not worry about my complexion or my figure. And I can ignore all those society grande dames, too.'

She laughed at the amazement on Nancy's face. 'Oh, if you ask, they'll tell you I've gone to pot. And I have, too. Mr. Leach was a wonderful husband, but while he was alive I had to keep myself to please him. I did, of course. Kept my figure slim and dressed right and went to the opera openings. But now that he's gone, God love him, I can do what I want. No more opera for me. Sure you won't have a chocolate?'

'Thank you, no. I came actually because . . . ' She hesitated.

'Because you were curious about the jade pieces being stolen, same as everyone is, and you thought I might be able to shed some light.'

'Well, yes, that's pretty much it.'

'Sit down. Yes, that's a comfortable chair. Hasn't it occurred to you, child, that I might be the thief?'

Nancy, sitting in one of the silk chairs, flushed a little. 'I hardly think that's likely.'

'But it's quite likely, don't you see? I'm a prime suspect. Obviously this isn't just some ordinary thief, since nothing else was taken. It's got to be a collector, and most likely, someone who had one of the jade pieces and wanted the rest of the collection. Well, there are only two of us left who haven't been robbed, me and that gentleman in Seattle.'

'I hadn't thought of it that way.'

'Well, you can bet your bottom dollar the police have. In a way, it will almost be a relief if mine gets stolen too. Then I won't have to worry about it, one way or another.' She chuckled and sat forward a little on the chaise longue. 'But I'm not making it easier for them, either. I've hired a guard, and I've brought the green man up here with me. If they want it, they'll have to move me out of this chair — and what with the weight I've put on, that's going to take some doing, wouldn't you say?'

There was a tap on the door and the maid came in. She looked a trifle piqued over something. 'Begging your pardon, ma'am,' she said from the doorway, 'but that guard gentleman has said I'll have to go to the store for him.' Her tone of voice said plainly that she did not think she should have to go.

Mrs. Leach, however, was of a different opinion. 'Well, dear, if it's something he needs, he can hardly go himself, can he, and guard me? You just do as the man wants for a few days, till all this nonsense blows over.' She turned back to Nancy. 'We just hired this young man. The insurance company called and said I ought to have somebody, and unless I had someone in mind, they'd be happy to send a man around. Tell the truth, I wouldn't have hired him otherwise; he looks like one of those hippies. But there, I suppose I'm being prejudiced unfairly.'

The maid had lingered at the door. When her mistress paused, she said to Nancy, 'He also said he'd like to see you on your way out, miss.'

Nancy looked puzzled, but Mrs. Leach quickly provided the explanation. 'There, you see — he wants to question you and see your credentials, I expect. I can't say he's not doing a bang-up job.'

'Well, as a matter of fact, I suppose I might as well be going now,' Nancy said, standing. 'I had simply hoped you might be able to give me some clue . . . but of course, I'm no detective.'

'Well, you come again, any time.' Mrs. Leach did not bother to get up. 'And tell your aunt I'm sorry about her loss. Isn't it lucky I didn't sell to her when she wanted me to? We'd have lost all the pieces, wouldn't we?'

The maid lingered to escort Nancy downstairs. 'The security man keeps a room off the kitchen,' she said. 'It's just at the end of the hall there. I've got to hurry to the drugstore, if I want to get back in time to catch my TV show.'

'I can find my own way, thank you,' Nancy said with a smile.

The maid hurried off toward the front door, and Nancy turned and walked toward the rear. She had been amused by her meeting with Mrs. Leach, but she knew no more than she had before.

Except, she amended, Mrs. Leach's theory that one of the collectors was behind the robberies. And if that were the case, then it was a matter of simple deduction to charge the man in Seattle — unless she wanted to accept the possibility that Mrs. Leach was the culprit, and she seriously doubted that.

She pushed open the door to the kitchen. 'Hello?' she called.

The man had been standing by the wall behind the door, so that she did not see him until she had stepped into the room and he had moved to close the door, at the same time blocking her exit.

'You wanted to see me?'

She turned and when she saw him her heart skipped a beat. It was like one of those nightmares that occurs again and again, with variations, but always with the same basic theme.

Here, once again, was her bearded man — wearing a blue uniform instead of his patched jeans, but the same man nonetheless, with his long, reddish-brown hair and even the sunglasses that concealed his eyes.

'You?' she gasped, backing away from him.

He stepped out from the door towards

her. 'This time,' he said hoarsely, 'I'm going to kill you.'

He blocked the door through which she had entered. There were two other doors, one at the far end of the kitchen and obviously leading to the backyard, and the other, partially open, to a storage room, but she could not hope to reach either of the doors before he seized her.

A large round table stood in the center of the room. As he came toward her she dodged his hand and ran around the table to face him across it.

He swore loudly and came after her. Again she ducked his hand and ran, once more facing him across the width of the table.

Her mind was racing frantically, trying to think of an escape. She was sure the maid was gone by now, sent on an errand obviously intended to get her out of the way while the bearded man dealt with the 'visitor', whose name he had no doubt gotten from the maid.

So far as Nancy knew, Mrs. Leach was the only other person in the house. Would she even hear if Nancy screamed? And if she did, was there anything she could do? She wouldn't even be able to get down here to the kitchen before the man had finished what he intended, and even if some miracle brought her here in time, what could she do against this strong young man?

The two of them continued their deadly game of tag around the table, dodging and panting, neither of them speaking. The only sound was the sound of their feet on the tile floor and the rasp of their breathing.

He lunged, reaching across the table in a desperate attempt to grab her. His hand missed, and he fell across the table. In the moment while he was off balance she sprang toward the closet door, the open one. She hadn't time to make a plan, except the desperate chance to escape his reaching hands.

She made it to the door, into the dark room beyond, and even as he was charging around the table toward her she slammed the door, and the spring lock clicked into place.

He slammed his fist against the door,

banging hard on it, and then the knob rattled fiercely. She was in darkness, but she could hear him, and hear his quick hard breathing on the other side of the door. She stood in darkness except for a crack of light that came in under the door and prayed that he would not be able to force the door open.

The banging stopped; seconds dragged by. Then she heard a muttered oath, and the sound of footsteps going away.

She leaned against the door and put a hand to her throat. Had he really gone away? Dared she chance an attempt to break for the rear door? Or might he be waiting just outside, having pretended to leave?

She hadn't the courage to make the dash for the rear door; but at the same time, she did not know just what she could do. There was no way that she could summon help from here. There were no windows, and the door was the only opening.

It was stalemate. Beyond the door was nothing but silence.

Surely the maid would not be gone more than a few minutes. She would be coming back soon. Unless he meant to do them all in, he would have to make a break for it soon. He couldn't just leave Nancy locked in the storage closet with people coming and going in the house.

It seemed as if she waited hours. All of her old childish fears of the dark came back to haunt her. She thought she heard all sorts of sounds, things moving in the dark beside her. A board creaked, and for an instant she thought that the bearded man had somehow gotten into the closet with her.

Her hammering heart persisted. It was no use trying to reason with a childhood fear. She was terrified sitting here in this tiny closet of darkness, and with each passing second her terror was growing.

She would have to try an escape; it was worth the risk to seize the chance, however slim.

She went to the door, pressing her ear to it, and listened. She could not say how long she had been here — perhaps five minutes, perhaps twenty, perhaps an hour. Once or twice she had thought she heard muffled sounds in the house, but she could not say what was real and what was imagination.

She put a hand to the lock and turned it as slowly and as silently as she was able. She held it at its far turn, waiting for a hand to seize the doorknob and try to open the door.

Nothing.

Finally, she pushed the door open a crack, her breath held, her heart in her throat.

Still nothing happened. No one sprang forward to seize the door and fling it open. The kitchen, what she could see of it in the opening, was empty and still.

She opened the door all the way. There was no one in the room. The door to the hall was closed. The one to the outside was only a few feet away.

She stepped into the kitchen, headed for the rear door and freedom.

She froze at the sound of footsteps in the hall — heavy, masculine steps. For a second or two she could not make her feet move; they felt as if they had put down roots into the tile floor. Terror held her to the spot.

She moved at last, almost too late, springing for the door that led to the outside, and hopefully to escape.

At the same moment someone stepped up to the door from outside, a man's bulky shape blocking the light through the frosted glass.

Nancy stopped in her tracks. As she did so, the door from the hall swung open noisily behind her.

12

She whirled about, a sense of doom sweeping over her.

It was not the bearded man who stood in the doorway; it was a policeman, his dark uniform looking like something straight from heaven to her frightened eyes.

'Oh, thank heaven,' she cried, her voice breaking on a sob. Another policeman had appeared behind the first. She would have run across the room and flung herself into the arms of the first man, except that he looked so stern she could hardly imagine him opening his arms to her.

'Who are you?' he asked gruffly. She saw that he had his gun drawn, and something about his manner was like a dash of cold water.

'I'm Nancy Dunbar,' she stammered. 'I came to see Mrs. Leach. But never mind that. There's a man here, dressed in a guard's uniform, but he's here to steal

Mrs. Leach's jade figurine. She thinks he was sent by her insurance company, but that was only a trick and . . . oh.' She realized she was babbling, took a deep breath, and started again.

'If we could go up to see Mrs. Leach,' she suggested, trying to smile. The man was looking at her so strangely, as if he thought she was the thief. But of course if the maid hadn't come back yet, they might well think that.

'Mrs. Leach is dead,' the policeman said bluntly.

She took a step backward. She felt as if he had slapped her. For a moment her mind went blank.

'Dead?'

'Strangled. Now, let's start over. Who are you and what are you doing here?'

* * *

Polly Dunbar was on the verge of hysteria, a new experience for her and a totally frightening one. She felt as if she had been running a puppet show, making the figures in the show do as she wanted, pulling the strings; and suddenly she had discovered that her puppets were alive and had wills of their own. The strings had been torn from her hands and she no longer was in control. Now it was she who was on a string.

She faced the man with the beard and realized that the power she had thought she held over him was an illusion. He was no longer hers to control. Indeed, it was he who was trying to control her.

'You're insane,' she said in a thin, shaky voice. 'When I hired you, I made it plain that all I wanted was the jade figures. I never wanted any of this. Certainly I didn't want murder.'

He looked unmoved by her remarks. 'I told you, things got messed up. Your niece showed up and I had to get the jade fast and go. I had to just take it, and I couldn't very well say to that Leach woman, excuse me, I want that figurine you've got hidden under the cushion in that chair your sitting in, would you mind letting me take it? Oh, and don't report it to the police, please?'

'But you didn't have to kill her,' Polly

almost screamed.

'Didn't I? How else do you think I was going to get it? Anyway, she could identify me.'

'But she's not the only one who can identify you,' Polly said.

'Well now, that's true,' he said with a nasty grin. 'But you can hardly point a finger, since you're the one who hired me. And what did you think I was going to do with him anyway?' He jerked his head toward the chair in which Harvey Blair was tied.

'That's kidnapping, on top of everything else,' he went on when she did not answer. 'That's a federal offense. Once we kidnapped him, there wasn't much difference whether we committed murder.'

Horror filled her mouth with bile. She looked across the room, and for the first time found herself meeting Harvey Blair's gaze.

'I — I didn't think . . . '

'Didn't you? Well I did. And so did the police. You and I are in it up to our sweet necks together. But you don't have to worry; I've done all the dirty work and I'll keep on doing it. All you got to come up with is money. And I need it now, to get out of town. We've finished here anyway. You got all those figurines except the one in Seattle. What you're going to do is, you're going to bring me a quarter of a million. That's a little more than we agreed upon, I'll admit, but things have gotten rougher than we planned originally. And I'll take the money and just disappear. And later, when things have quieted down, we'll think about getting that seventh piece.'

She put out a hand to the plastic-topped table to steady herself. 'I don't want it,' she said. 'I don't want any of them. Not after all this.'

'No?' he gave a low, vicious laugh. 'Getting a conscience finally, are you? Well, it's too late, lady. You can't undo what we've done. You can't bring that old bag back to life. All you can do is get me that money and quick, and then go back to your mansion and play dumb, and everything will be fine in a little while.'

She forced herself to look into the man's gleaming eyes, and saw what she should have seen long before — violence and death and evil without mercy. 'Yes,' she said in a whisper. 'Yes, I'll get the money. It will take me perhaps a day; banks can be difficult about these things. I'll get it to you as soon as I can.'

'That's better.' He studied her intently. 'Yeah, you're okay now. For a minute there I thought you was going to flip on me. But you look like your old self now.'

'I only want to be done with all this. I'm sick of the entire affair.' She gathered her purse and her gloves, avoiding having to look even for an instant toward the man in the chair. 'I'll be back either tonight, or first thing in the morning.' She started toward the door.

'See that you are.'

She felt as if she were walking on eggs, sure that if he could see her face he would never let her leave, and it was only by a supreme effort of will that she was able to walk slowly, without running. At the door she said, without looking back at him, 'Tomorrow, then.'

She went down the stairs slowly, each step an agony. Her legs were trembling so that twice she nearly fell. Her head was swimming, and her breath came in little shuddering gasps.

She knew one of her spells was coming on. She fought against it, fighting for breath, fighting back the curtain of darkness that threatened to descend upon her.

She must get home first. She must tell Nancy everything.

Nancy. Her name had not been mentioned, but she had realized up there in that filthy room that he meant to kill Nancy too. And for the first time in her life, Polly Dunbar's heart had been touched by an unselfish emotion. She had realized that she loved her niece.

The rest of it she might have been able to live with — the murder of that silly old woman, even the murder of Harvey Blair. She might have been able in time to suit her thinking to those, and to console herself that the green men were hers at last, the dream of her lifetime. And after all, her conscience would not have had long to bother her. A few months more, at the most.

But she could not let him murder

Nancy, as she knew beyond any doubt he meant to do. No matter what it cost, she must prevent that. If it meant telling the police everything, she must do it.

A wave of sick dizziness rushed through her. She reached the sidewalk and put a hand to the door jamb, breathing deeply and fighting the sinking feeling. She must reach home to warn Nancy. After that, it didn't matter about the rest.

★　★　★

It had been like a nightmare. The police, questioning, plainly not believing her story of being locked in the storage closet. The maid, who had come back to find her mistress dead and the house apparently empty, had been convinced that Nancy had been the guilty one.

Nancy had been taken handcuffed to the police station, and there Detective Davis had come to question her. Dully, wearily, she had repeated her story again and again. Whether Davis had finally begun to believe her or not, she did not know, but at last he had gone out of the

195

room and when he came back, Tom was with him.

'It's all right,' Tom whispered when she had run sobbing into his arms. 'It's all right. No one's going to throw you into the Bastille.'

Finally he had taken her home. She did not know if she was still under suspicion or what, and at the moment did not care. She wanted only to be among familiar surroundings; to shed the feeling of helplessness that had engulfed her from that first glimpse of the bearded man in Mrs. Leach's kitchen.

They were at the house now. Aunt Polly was out but Ellen, as cool and efficient as ever, had hurriedly brought brandies, and announced that she would have fresh tea ready in a minute.

'I've got to go back to the station,' Tom said. 'I promised Davis I'd bring you home and come back.'

She managed a wry smile. 'Am I still suspect?'

'More or less. I promised I'd take full responsibility for you. Will you be all right now?'

'Yes, don't worry. Ellen is here, and Aunt Polly will be back soon, I'm sure. And if need be, I'll push the furniture against the doors for a barricade.'

He left, promising to be in touch in the morning. By the time she had finished the brandy and two cups of the tea, and had soaked in a warm tub, Nancy had begun to feel more like herself. She felt quite weary with all that had happened, and painfully sorry for the cheerful Mrs. Leach.

She had spent most of the afternoon at the police station, and now the rooms were growing dusky with the approach of night. She had just gotten out of a chair to turn on the living room lights when she heard the sound of a key in the front door, and a moment later Aunt Polly came in.

The woman who came to the doorway of the living room was not, however, the calm, self-possessed woman that Nancy was accustomed to seeing. She was a wild-eyed demon, her hair in disarray, her shoulders shaking with the effort of her breathing.

Nancy took a step toward her, alarmed

at once by her aunt's frantic appearance. 'Aunt Polly, what's wrong?' she asked. 'Are you ill?'

Polly's hand reached out toward her niece. She tried to say something, but seemed unable to bring the words past her throat.

'Nancy . . . ' was all she managed before she collapsed into Nancy's arms.

★　★　★

With Ellen's help, Nancy got her aunt to bed and summoned Doctor Williams. That genial man came promptly as usual and administered a sedative.

'She seems to have had some sort of a bad shock,' he said to Nancy. 'Any idea what brought it on?'

'No, she seemed to be trying to tell me something when she came in. She looked — well, wild, I'd say, if you understand what I mean. Frantic with — I don't know what. Fear, I suppose.'

'She didn't get anything out?'

'Not a word except my name.'

He put his things back into his bag and

snapped it shut. 'If she really was trying to tell you something,' he said, 'something so important that it brought on this attack, it will probably stay with her. I mean, when she wakes up. She will probably want nothing else but to finish delivering whatever her message was.'

'But do you think it could be anything really important?'

'She thought it was.'

When he had gone, Nancy stood for a moment in the downstairs hall, thinking. Ellen came out from the kitchen.

'How is she?' she asked.

'Quiet.' Nancy came to a decision. 'Ellen, I'm going to stay in Aunt Polly's room until she awakens. Would you mind awfully bringing me something up to eat?'

'I was about to ask if you couldn't use something. I'll bring it right up.'

Settled into the big chaise longue in Aunt Polly's room, Nancy thought back over the day's events. Had Aunt Polly heard of the death of Mrs. Leach and the theft of the sixth green man? Perhaps that was what had brought on the attack.

Ellen brought in a tray with supper,

setting it on the little dressing table by the chaise longue, and went out again. Nancy, her appetite suddenly whetted by the scent of food, ate with gusto. She washed it down with the wine Ellen had thoughtfully put on the tray.

When she had finished, and was sipping hot coffee, she felt better able to sort out her thoughts. This latest robbery and the ugly murder had darkened the picture considerably for her father and for herself. Detective Davis might have believed her story of how she had come to be in Mrs. Leach's house at the time, but she doubted it; and she was sure, too, that he was convinced she was lying when she had insisted she still did not know of her father's whereabouts.

There was one consolation to the whole affair. The seventh of the jade figures, the only one that had not yet been stolen, was in Seattle. She had no intention of going to Seattle in the near future — perhaps never, until she knew what had really happened to the green men. And if and when that last figure was stolen too, then some of the cloud of suspicion hanging over her would be removed.

Nancy slept for a while, curled up on the chaise. It was after midnight when she was awakened by a sound from Aunt Polly's bed. Awake at once, Nancy went to the bed to find her aunt's eyes open. For a moment aunt Polly looked around frantically. Then her gaze settled on her niece.

'Nancy,' she said in a strained and urgent whisper.

'It's all right, Aunt Polly. I'm here.'

Aunt Polly's hand fluttered in the air as if she were trying to reach up for something. Nancy realized her aunt was motioning for her to lean closer, and she bent down over the figure on the bed.

Aunt Polly was straining, trying to speak. She said faintly, 'The shack . . . '

She tried to say more but the effort was too great. She exhaled loudly, closed her eyes, and sank once more into unconsciousness.

Nancy straightened up, running a finger through her hair. She frowned down at the unconscious figure on the bed.

The shack was a cabin that Aunt Polly

had in the redwood forests above San Francisco. It had been so long since they had been there, or since Nancy had even heard it mentioned, that she had virtually forgotten about it, and would not have been surprised to learn that her aunt no longer owned the property.

Nancy had a dim memory that for a time the cabin had been rented out to someone, or perhaps to vacationers, and then it had dropped from her aunt's conversation altogether, and had been all but forgotten by Nancy herself.

What significance could the cabin have now?

An idea leapt into her mind. The shack would be an ideal place for someone to hide out. At once she thought of her father. If the shack had been in the family for a long time, he too might know of it; and if he had needed a place to hide out, it was possible he had gone there, and that Aunt Polly had somehow discovered his whereabouts. Perhaps, in fact, her father had been trying to reach her; perhaps he wanted her to come to the cabin, and Aunt Polly had been trying to deliver that message.

She glanced at her watch. It was almost twelve thirty, but she knew she would not sleep any more this night until she had learned for herself what was at the cabin. She left her aunt's room and stole along the halls to Ellen's room, tapping lightly at the door.

13

Ellen sat up in bed, startled at being roused in this way. 'What is it?'

'Ellen, the old cabin in the woods, do you know of it?'

'The shack? Lord, yes. Mr. Dunbar — your aunt's father — used to go up there all the time. I haven't even heard it mentioned in years though. What on earth . . . ?'

Nancy was too excited to want a long discussion now. 'Do you think you could draw me a map to find it?'

'A map? Well I suppose if I had a regular map, I could mark it for you. But . . . '

'There are maps in the library. Oh, Ellen, I haven't time to explain now. Please, while I'm dressing, would you get one of the maps and mark it for me?'

Ellen gave a sigh of exasperation, but she was already throwing back the covers and getting out of bed. 'I suppose I can, but I don't mind saying it seems a peculiar time to be thinking about that old place, after all these years.'

'Yes, isn't it?' Nancy ran down the hall to her own room, where she hurriedly shed her dressing gown and dressed in street clothes — a warm, long skirt and a sweater. She took a final look in on Aunt Polly, to find her sleeping quietly again.

She found Ellen in the library, with a map, the route in red ink. 'I hope your memory's good,' Nancy said, folding the map to drop it in the large purse she was carrying.

'Oh, that's the right route. But I didn't mark the map. Someone else had already done that.'

Nancy's pulse quickened. Then someone else had gone to the cabin recently, probably Aunt Polly. That certainly must mean that there was something hidden there — something or someone waiting for her arrival.

'I'll be back by morning,' she said. 'Keep an eye on my aunt.'

She took the Bentley. It was late at

night, traffic having thinned out to a trickle, but the fog made driving a slow process. She saw an all-night service station and stopped for gas and to have the tires checked. Although of course the area she was driving into had no doubt been built up considerably since she had been there as a child, it was still sufficiently isolated that she did not want to have any sort of car troubles on the way. As she left San Francisco driving north, the fog thinned out and she was able to make better time for a while.

Almost at once she was in pine forests. There were only a very few other cars out. She could see headlights in the rear-view mirror, but far enough behind that the glare did not bother her; and from time to time a car passed the other way, heading into the city.

She watched for her turnoff and she left the main highway for a much narrower road that twisted up into the hills. She passed through a small town, now asleep and without a soul stirring on the streets. As she left the village, she passed a police cruiser and saw the driver look after her, but she had not been speeding and he did not follow her.

She was getting drowsy. She had been driving about an hour; and although the distance she had travelled was not great, and the pine forests outside the car were silent and dark, they seemed light years away from the bustle and noise of San Francisco.

When she saw a safe turnoff, she pulled off the road for a break. She found matches and cigarettes in her purse and, lighting one, climbed out of the car to stretch her legs a bit.

The air was cool and sweet with the scent of pine and juniper and sage. What had seemed at first to be silence was not silence at all. There was the sighing of leaves and boughs in the breeze, and the whisper of winged creatures overhead. An owl startled her with a sudden shrill cry, and the bushes near the road rustled as some animal moved through them.

Her nerves were too on-edge and she was impatient to finish her trip. She ground the cigarette out carefully on the road surface and got into the car again.

She did not have very far to go now. She resisted an impulse to drive fast and kept her foot steady on the accelerator.

By the time she saw the sign for her turn-off, hidden in a tangle of growth, she was too far past. She hit the brake, coming to a stop a few yards beyond the gravel road, and backed up to make the turn.

The going now was definitely slower. She was in the redwood forests, with only an occasional cabin to indicate that people did indeed come this way. The road curved often and sharply, and the gravel surface made driving difficult.

She found the lane with no difficulty, a narrow dirt track. She was a little disappointed to see no lights at the cabin. Of course, it was the middle of the night. If her father were here, he certainly would be asleep now, and he would not be likely to have all the lights blazing anyway.

She turned off the engine and sat for a moment, trying to will herself calm. Finally she stepped out of the car, into the crisp night air. The path up to the door was buried under pine needles, making her progress silent and ghostly.

She tried the door and found it locked. Ellen had told her the key was always kept in the planter box by the north window. She found it and let herself in quietly, pausing just inside the door, not sure just what she should do. There might be someone here other than her father.

'Is anyone here?' she asked softly, and then again more loudly, 'Anyone here?'

No answer. She found a light switch, and the overhead light filled the room with a yellowish glare. She stepped into the room and closed the door.

Someone had been here. Several cigarettes had been put out in an ashtray, and in the kitchen the coffee in the cup on the counter had not completely dried up.

She paused at the bedroom door to say, 'Hello.'

There was no one in the bed, nor did it look as if anyone had slept in it for a long time. She went to the closet door and opened it, and caught her breath in surprise.

She had come to the cabin hoping to find one man. Instead, she had found six men. Jade-green, they stood in a neat row on the closet shelf.

14

The immortals stared back at Nancy, their pale surfaces gleaming in the light like the waters of some mysterious ocean. With a trembling hand Nancy reached for one of the figurines and took it down from the shelf, running her fingers over the sleek surface.

Yes, there was no doubt, these were the green men. She recognized the three that had belonged to her aunt; the other three were new to her, but equally beautiful. In those sculptured faces, so delicately modeled, one seemed to see centuries of wisdom, of resignation, of beauty. She felt dazed by her discovery.

She went back into the living room. There was a makeshift bar on the kitchen counter; she poured herself some brandy and, taking that with her, curled up in one of the chairs. She needed to get some sort of order in the whirling confusion of her thoughts.

The green men were here — not only Aunt Polly's three, but the other three that had been stolen. And Aunt Polly had known they were here. Why else send her on this quest to find them?

How had Aunt Polly known they were here? Had she come to the shack herself for some reason — and when? Had she discovered them herself by accident? And if so, then the question still remained, how had they gotten here? It was begging too much of coincidence to think that some burglar, having stolen the figures from the owners scattered about the country, could have chosen this very cabin by chance.

Somehow, Aunt Polly was involved in the theft.

It was incredible. Why on earth would Aunt Polly be involved in robbery, when she was already frightfully wealthy? She had all that she would ever need or want.

Except, Nancy amended almost at once. Except the remaining green men.

She could not have known her aunt all these years without knowing the importance Aunt Polly attached to 'things' — possessions. And of all her possessions, none were more important to her than the green men. They were her treasures; and they were incomplete. Three of a set of seven. How often had Aunt Polly bemoaned the fact that she had only three when she wanted the complete set, hers, to own?

Nancy sat and sipped the brandy, and pondered these things, and the night went by. When finally she got up from the chair, stretching herself sleepily, dawn was not far off.

She had made up her mind to take the green men with her. If Aunt Polly were conscious and able to talk when she got back to the house, she would confront her and demand to know the whole story. And if she were still unconscious, then she would turn the green men over to Tom and allow him to unravel the mystery of their presence here. Those cool green figures had already caused enough heartache and tragedy and confusion. She wanted to be done with them.

She found some old newspapers in the wastebasket and shredded several sheets for wrapping. Then she wrapped each of the figures individually and placed them in the brown bag she had unearthed in the kitchen.

Finally, carefully turning off the lights and locking the door, she let herself out and walked through the thinning darkness to the Bentley, carrying a fortune in priceless objets d'art in a grocery sack.

* * *

A telephone rang. Detective Davis reached for the instrument and barked his name at it. He listened for a few minutes, grunting occasionally. 'No,' he said finally into the mouthpiece, 'stay with her just to see that she gets back to the house. Then hightail it in here.'

He replaced the receiver and pivoted slightly in his chair to face Tom Farroday, seated on the other side of the desk.

'We've got the jade figures,' Davis said. 'Your girlfriend is on her way back to San Francisco with them.'

Tom sat forward on his chair edge, startled. 'She didn't have them, surely?' he said.

Davis shook his head. 'No, they were in a cabin north of here. That's where she was heading when she left the house earlier. I had a man following her. He tailed her up to this cabin in the redwoods, then got out of his car and snuck up for a look-see. He was looking in a window when she opened a closet door and there were the jade pieces. He says she looked as surprised as he was.'

Tom exhaled loudly and leaned back in his chair. 'Who does this cabin belong to, do you know?'

'Not yet, but we will soon enough,' Davis said. 'My man is going to follow her back just to be sure she's going home, then report back here. I'm going to have her picked up again. I want to know whose cabin that is, and what made her go up there. Someone must have sent her.'

'It won't be necessary to have her picked up. I'll bring her here.'

He got up and walked around the desk to the telephone. He and Davis had been kicking the case around for hours now, but he had not known until now that

Davis had a man watching Nancy. He would not have thought it necessary, since he had believed she was safely in bed, not somewhere north of the city discovering the missing pieces of jade for them.

The phone rang at least a dozen times before a sleepy and angry voice answered it. 'Ellen?' Tom said into the instrument. 'Sorry to call so late. This is Mr. Farroday. Yes, I know Nancy's not there. She'll be getting back there in roughly an hour and a half. Now listen — this is urgent. As soon as she comes in I want you to have her call me at — ' He paused to squint at the number on the phone, and gave it to her. 'This is urgent, got that? I want her to call the very first thing, before she does anything else.

'When she calls,' he said, hanging up and turning back to Davis, 'I'll ask her to come down here, or we can go to the house to talk, whichever you prefer.'

'Great.' Davis bit the end off a fresh cigar. 'I still wish I knew where her dad is. That's who I thought she was going to meet.'

Harvey Blair was on a journey of his own. It was only yards long, yet so far it had taken him as long as it had taken his daughter to drive the miles to the cabin — and he was not yet at his destination.

He was travelling toward the plastic-topped kitchen table at the far end of the room from where he had been seated. He had started a couple of hours before, when Marston had gone out.

He did not want to think of Marston, or what his errand had been. That it was something extraordinary, he was sure. Why else shave off his beard and cut his hair to a rather conservative length? Why don a gray suit and a shirt and tie, until he looked like a modest businessman instead of a hippie?

Just before leaving, Marston had used the wicked-looking hunting knife to saw off a piece of bread from a stale-looking loaf. He had chewed on the hard bread, and had chuckled to himself at something he was contemplating. He waved the knife at Harvey and said, 'Yeah, and when I'm

216

back, I'll take care of the both of you.' Finished with the bread, he had stuck the knife in the remaining loaf and had gone out.

Harvey had listened as his footsteps faded down the stairs. Then Harvey had begun his journey, struggling with all the faint strength he had left to drag himself and his chair across the room to the table, to where the knife stood embedded in the loaf of bread.

In all that time, stopping every several minutes to suck badly needed breath into his lungs, he had made it halfway across the room.

15

The sky was pale gray as Nancy approached the Golden Gate Bridge, and dawn was just breaking by the time she drove up the hill toward her aunt's home. It was a rare quiet hour for the city. Hardly anyone was stirring. In the time since she had left the bridge, Nancy had seen perhaps one other car.

She was tired. She'd had only an hour or so of catnapping in Aunt Polly's room earlier this evening; and on top of that, all the unaccustomed driving that had left her shoulders aching. She longed for a hot bath and a soft bed. Perhaps after all she would rest before she tried to unravel the knotted threads of the mystery of the jade figurines. Even an hour or so would help. Anyway, it was too early to call anyone — Tom, or even Detective Davis.

The policeman in the car behind her had dropped back several blocks lest in the morning's light she notice him.

Probably, though, she was too tired to be observant of a car trailing several blocks behind her. He did not need to be close on her heels. He felt reasonably certain she was headed home, and needed only to confirm that.

Up the hill her brake lights came on and she turned slowly into the drive. She left her car blocking the sidewalk and got out to open the garage door.

He did not even have to risk being spotted driving past. His orders were to see where she was going and then report back to Davis. He turned at the next corner and headed toward the station.

*   *   *

'Miss Dunbar?'

Nancy paused in the act of closing the car door, and turned surprised eyes on the man just getting out of the car parked on the street. She did not know him — a tall man in a gray suit.

'Yes,' she said, one hand still on the car door.

He walked across to her. There was

219

something familiar about him, but she was tired, and her mind would not identify what it was.

'My name is Marston, I work with Tom Farroday.' He smiled in an apologetic way. 'He sent me to get you.'

'To get me? What for?'

'There's someone he wants you to identify if you can. He said to come and get you and bring you right back. I've been waiting for you to come home.'

'But it's only . . . ' She glanced at her watch. 'It's six o'clock in the morning.'

'He said it's very important, miss. He said you'd come right along if you knew that.'

She sighed wearily. If Tom thought it was important . . . and he surely must, to have sent someone for her at this hour.

'I'll just run inside for a minute,' she said. He seemed about to object and she said impatiently, 'Yes, yes, I know it's important. But another minute or two can't matter that much. I'll be right back.'

He looked displeased, but he said nothing more to stop her. She went quickly up the steps and let herself in the front door.

She was splashing cold water on her face in the bathroom when, to her surprise, Ellen tapped at the door. 'Begging your pardon, miss,' she said, looking as if she hadn't slept much more than Nancy, 'but Mr. Farroday called during the night. He says would you call him back whenever you get in — it's very urgent.'

Nancy felt actually a little relieved to hear the message. It had occurred to her that the man outside had shown her no identification, and she had wondered if she ought to ask for it. Now that she knew Tom was trying to reach her urgently, it seemed it was all right.

'No need now,' she said, running a comb through her hair. 'He sent a man to wait for me. I was just leaving again with him. How is Aunt Polly?'

'Still sleeping. You won't be wanting breakfast then?'

'I wish I could,' Nancy said with a note of anguish in her voice. Just now she would have traded several years of her life

221

for a cup of fresh coffee.

She brushed her teeth — that at least made her feel fresher — and hurried down the stairs. She had been trying to decide what to do about the green men. She had nearly told Tom's associate about them and given them to him before, but she had decided against that. If it were possible, she wanted to ask Aunt Polly about them first. So she had left the figures where they were, locked in the trunk of the Bentley. And there they would just have to stay for the present, since the waiting detective was sure to be curious if she opened the trunk to take the sack out. And of course, with the figures in the trunk, she had no intention of being separated from the Bentley any more than she had to be.

'I want to take my own car,' she said to the waiting detective when she came outside.

'It'd be easier if we just went in mine.'

She was in no mood for long argument. She let herself into her car. 'There's no traffic out this early. I'll have no trouble following you.'

He seemed about to argue, but apparently a glance at the stubborn set of her chin convinced him otherwise. He shrugged and said, 'Makes no difference to me.'

He walked briskly back to the Volkswagen he had been in before. Watching him, Nancy thought again that there was something familiar about the man. Had Tom introduced her to him at some time? She tried to recall, but she was just too tired to think clearly. Oh, what she would have given for an hour's sleep!

The Volkswagen pulled into the street and waited for her. She started up the Bentley, backing into the street. The Volkswagen set off, and she followed it.

Ordinarily the telephone did not ring much. But it seemed to Ellen that, on this one night at least, it had been making up for days of silence.

'Hello,' she said gruffly into the mouthpiece. When she heard who was calling, she said rather sharply, 'Yes, Mr. Farroday, she did get home, just a few minutes ago. She left right away with that man of yours.'

The voice on the other end of the line was several seconds in asking, 'What man?'

'The one you had waiting outside for her. She came in and combed her hair, and left to come see you.'

At the station, Tom replaced the receiver with shaky hands. 'Someone met her at the house,' he said to Davis. 'Not one of your men, I take it?'

Davis shook his head.

'Good thing that man of yours is tailing her,' Tom said.

The phone rang. Davis answered it and grunted several times before he replaced it. 'That was Meyers,' he said, fixing his cool gaze on Farroday's face. 'The man I had tailing the girl. He saw her home, and is reporting back in. He's outside now.'

For a long moment the two men only looked at one another. Then Davis again reached for the phone.

'Pete,' he said into it, 'I want to put out an APB on a gray Bentley.'

16

Nancy had expected vaguely to go to a police station, but the man called Marston drove instead to the fringes of the Haight-Ashbury district. About them the city was just beginning to stir: the early-morning people were coming out of their doors, some of them; those who worked early hours were on the streets. Women in wrappers came to their doors for the morning paper.

In Haight-Ashbury, though, where night life was the rule, no one stirred.

Ahead of her the Volkswagen slowed; its driver signaled toward a parking place. She stopped and backed into it, while he took one a few yards further on.

She was really feeling her exhaustion now, and the strain of staying up all night. She did a poor job of parking. By the time she had pulled out again to try a second time, Marston was parked and walking back toward her. She shot him a resentful glance and tugged at the wheel of the Bentley.

She got it in this time, glad that she didn't have to show herself up as completely inept with the cold-eyed detective waiting. She fumbled for her purse on the seat, realized she had forgotten to switch off the engine, and reached for the key. Marston opened the door for her.

She dropped the keys. Deliberately. And as she bent down, groping about the floor of the car for them, she could almost feel the blood draining from her face, and knew that it must be as white as a sheet.

She'd had only a swift glance at Marston's hand, but she was not likely ever to forget that scar. She had seen it just a day ago, when he had told her he was going to kill her.

The long hair and the beard and even the sunglasses were gone, and she had never seen him dressed in a suit and tie, but this was her nemesis; she knew that in the flicker of an eye.

Her heart thumping, she tried to think what to do. She could not stay forever bent over in the seat, groping about on the floor of the car for the keys that she could see quite clearly by her right foot.

'I can't seem to find the keys,' she said, hoping her voice didn't sound as unnatural to him as it did to her.

'They're right there, by your foot.'

She 'found' the keys, picking them up in shaking fingers, and sat upright again.

'Lord,' she said, managing an embarrassed sounding laugh, 'I am getting absent-minded. I forgot my aunt was to have her medicine first thing this morning.'

He looked understandably surprised at this piece of makeshift intelligence. 'You'll only be a couple of minutes,' he said, swinging the door all the way open.

'I know, but the doctor said it's awfully important.'

'Tom Farroday said this was important too.'

'Well, yes.' She hesitated, frantically searching her mind for some excuse to get away from the man before he got those hands on her again; before he realized, as any fool must do from the fear in her eyes, that she had recognized him.

'I wonder, though,' she added, still hesitating inside the car, 'if I oughtn't find a phone and just call Ellen. Then I won't have to hurry back, don't you see.'

She had a notion that if she could only get him away from the car long enough for her to start it up and get out of the parking space . . . How long would that take? A minute? Two?

'Miss Blair,' he said, and the impatience in his voice was unmistakable, 'I wasn't supposed to tell you, but the man you're supposed to identify may be your father.'

She took in her breath in a rush and snapped her head around to look up at him. She met his cold eyes, and a shock wave of fear went through her. He was telling the truth about that, she was suddenly certain. She was as sure as she had ever been of anything that he had her father, probably just inside this house where they were parked.

'Is he . . . is he alive?'

He looked troubled. 'He's been hurt. Understand, we're not certain, not one hundred percent certain, that it is your father. If you'll just come with me.'

He put a hand into the car, taking hold of her arm gently but firmly, and she let him tug her out of the car. She got out numbly, following his lead, hardly hearing the slam of the car door behind her.

Her legs were unsteady, and not only from her lack of sleep and the long time she had spent in the car. She did not know what to do. She could not just run, even if she could get away from him, not knowing that her father might be a prisoner inside, dying or even dead; surely he would be dead if she ran. Yet the thought of accompanying this man into this house filled her with horror so that she could hardly manage to get one foot in front of the other.

Come into my parlor, said the spider to the fly. Her thoughts were a crazy jumble. This was probably the first time the fly had been escorted in by a spider with a solicitous hand at her elbow.

He opened a door onto a steep narrow flight of stairs, handing her in ahead of him, so that she had no choice but to go up the creaking stairs with him behind her.

The landing at the top had a single door, but still she paused. 'In here?'

'Yes.'

She turned the knob and pushed the door inward, stepping into the apartment. It was dim inside and for a moment she could not see much of anything. She blinked, looking slowly from left to right.

There was no one here. She took a step into the room, Marston following close after her.

17

Things happened then quite suddenly, so that even afterward everything was a blur.

Someone grabbed hold of her arm, hard. She thought at first it was Marston, but it wasn't. She was half-pulled, half-thrown forward, so that she staggered and might have fallen had she not put her hand up to the plastered wall to keep her balance.

She had a glimpse of a flash of light on metal, a knife blade arcing downward through the air. She gave a little squeal of fright; but the knife was for Marston, not her.

He gave a gasp of his own, more of surprise than pain, and staggered also, but in trying to sidestep he had thrown himself hard to the right. He fell across one of the chairs and went crashing to the floor. The table fell too, dishes and pots banging onto the floor.

The man with the knife sprang toward

Marston, and only then did Nancy realize it was her father. He still had the knife, and if he had not been so patently weak, or Marston had been a little less alert, the knife would no doubt this time have found a more serious target than the scant surface of one lifted forearm.

Marston was already scrambling out of the way, and as the hand with the knife came down, he seized the wrist, twisting. The knife clattered to the floor.

Nancy stepped back, pressing herself against the plastered surface of a wall, watching as the two men on the floor grappled in a life-and-death battle. She could see that it was Marston's fight. He was young and strong, and her father was obviously weak.

Marston flung the older man off of him as easily as if he were a rag doll. Harvey Blair groaned and tried to get up, but Marston had grabbed his ankle.

'Nancy, run!' Her father cried. 'Run!'

Every nerve in her body was telling her the same thing, urging her to bolt through that open door, down those creaking stairs to freedom. But she couldn't, and leave her father to that killer on the floor who even now had gotten himself atop the weaker man and was strangling him with those powerful hands.

Her father's hand felt about on the floor and found a frying pan that had been on the table when it fell. He got a desperate grip on the pan and brought it down across the back of Marston's head.

The fight was over. Marston fell motionless across her father.

'Oh Dad, Dad,' Nancy sobbed, running to help him get from under the unconscious man. Her father's face was ashen, his eyes black caverns of exhaustion. When he lifted a hand, she saw his wrists were torn and bleeding. She gasped involuntarily.

'I've been tied up,' he said with faltering breath. 'Had to cut myself loose.'

On the floor, Marston groaned and stirred.

'We've got to get out of here,' her father said. 'I can't manage him again.'

'The car's outside.'

She helped her father toward the door. He was even weaker now, as if he had summoned all of his strength for that battle with Marston, and now was only just able to walk with her help.

They managed the steps, slowly and a bit clumsily. The waiting Bentley was the most welcome sight she had ever seen. She got her father safely inside and ran around to the driver's side, slipping into the seat behind the wheel. Her hands shook so that she nearly dropped the keys trying to put the right one in the ignition. The big engine sprang to life.

As she tried to pull out of the parking space she heard a shout and saw Marston stagger out the door to the apartment. With another shout, he staggered toward them.

She backed into the car behind them, shifted gears again and pulled forward, trying to clear that fender in front. She still hadn't cut it.

Marston was at the car, reaching for the door handle. She stepped down on the gas and the big car sprang forward, neatly pushing that blocking fender out of the way with no more than a crunching sound, and they were in the street. She glanced back in the mirror. Marston ran after the car for a few feet. She watched him recede in the rear view mirror.

'Thank God,' she said in a whisper, shaking all over. 'Are you all right?'

'Yes,' he said. He obviously was not all right, though. He leaned weakly against the car door.

They came over the crest of a hill and saw that the street ahead was blocked for some construction project. The workmen were jockeying a pair of trucks around for position. A huge truck carrying a gigantic-looking cement mixer was backed across the street while another truck, a flatbed, backed out of a driveway. One of the construction workers stood in the street with a red flag, halting oncoming traffic.

'What can we do?' her father asked.

'For a minute or two, nothing. As soon as we can move, we'll go straight to the police station. If these men ever get their trucks straightened around.'

The driver of the flatbed was having some difficulty making it out of the drive-way. The construction site was surrounded by a high wooden fence with a narrow opening for the trucks to get through, but it was a close fit.

The driver got part way out, but the sides of his truck were scraping the fence. With much roaring of the engine and grinding of gears, he pulled forward again for another try.

In the rear-view mirror, Nancy saw a gray Volkswagen come over the hill and start down toward them, slowing as it approached the obstruction. She did not have to see the driver to guess who it was. She felt as if the bottom had dropped out of her stomach.

'He's caught up with us.'

Her father's head shot around, his dark eyes wide with alarm. The Volkswagen slowed as it approached a red van just behind the Bentley.

18

The flatbed truck scraped the wooden fence again.

'All these workmen,' Nancy said. 'Surely he wouldn't dare do anything here.'

'He's crazy. And desperate. He's liable to do anything.'

Marston got out of the Volkswagen. Nancy needed only one look at his face to realize her father was right. She honked the horn, trying to get the attention of the workmen. The man with the flag gave his head a shake and turned to say something to the driver of the cement truck. They were laughing, and she realized they thought her honking horn was a sign of impatience at having to wait. Marston loomed at the rear fender, his eyes wild.

In a near panic Nancy slammed her foot down on the gas pedal. The Bentley shot forward like a charging elephant, straight toward the man with the red flag.

His eyes went wide and the cigar he had been chewing on fell from his mouth, but fear held him rooted to the spot.

She yanked violently at the wheel and they leapt the curb. She clung to the wheel and aimed for the incredibly narrow space between a utility pole and that wooden fence.

Metal bent and squealed and there was only that tiny place to cross, between the cement truck and the flatbed truck, over that makeshift driveway. It was too small an opening, she thought frantically; surely it was too small. She had a glimpse of the truck backing up, coming toward the gate again. Of all the people on the scene, that driver was the only one who could not know what was happening.

Impatiently the driver gunned the motor. He hardly even needed to turn in his seat to look, he was so confident of himself this time.

He did turn his head to look, though, just as he was passing through the opening.

He had a glimpse of something gray shooting by. He saw, so fast it hardly registered, a terrified face turned his way. There was a ripping sound of metal being torn and the truck swayed with the impact of collision.

He hit the brakes hard and jumped out of the truck's cab, heading at a run toward the rear. He expected to see a car resting in a heap on the sidewalk. He was still completely in the dark as to what the car had been doing there anyway, rocketing by that opening just when he was backing out. Where the devil was the flagman, anyway? And what in the name of everything holy was a car doing driving along the sidewalk?

At the sidewalk he had just a glimpse of a gray car careening around a corner. It was impossible to say just what the car was. One entire side was a mass of crumpled metal. A rear fender had been torn loose, revealing the wheel-house and part of the car's underside, and the wheel at that fender looked like it would fall off any minute.

He was surprised the car was still moving. It disappeared around the corner, a fading screech warning that one of the fenders was rubbing a tire. He gave them maybe another block or two before the car gave out.

Some of the other men ran up. 'Sure was in a hurry, wasn't she?' the flagman said.

Everyone laughed, somewhat unsteadily. The driver of the cement truck yelled down, 'Hey, there's a guy back here, says he's a doctor and he's on an emergency call, has to get through here.'

⋆　⋆　⋆

Nancy couldn't tell how much of the shaking was in her hands and how much of it was the car. It kept wanting to fly away to the left, bouncing and bucking endlessly. She held so tightly to the steering wheel that her knuckles were white.

If only a policeman would come along, so she could risk stopping. Why, oh why couldn't a policeman appear now?

Something was squealing, and she thought she smelled burning rubber. She didn't know how many more blocks the car would hobble along. She must do something — something — but what?

She glanced in the rear-view mirror and saw a wisp of smoke coming from where the rear fender had been. She looked for someplace to pull into, someplace out of sight.

'Here he comes,' her father said.

She glanced toward the mirror and saw the Volkswagen rushing after them, at a speed several times theirs.

She gripped the steering wheel tighter still and floored the accelerator. The car seemed to shudder beneath her, like a great wounded beast trying to shake its rider. Then, as if gathering itself together, it sprang forward. The tire shrieked in protest, and a flame suddenly sparked into life.

They hit a trolley track and the Bentley skidded and threw itself sideways. Nancy was flung against the door, tugging at the steering wheel, trying to bring the swaying car around again. She had a blurred impression of a store front rushing at her, then swinging past her shoulder, and they were more or less straight again, on the wrong side of the road. The Volkswagen was close enough for her to see Marston's enraged expression. He was waving the gun at her now.

A car pulled out of a driveway, blocking her way before the driver saw her hurtling along on his side of the street. He hit his horn and it blared like a warning trumpet as she swerved and skidded, trying to get around him. The Bentley was on fire now, orange and blue flames flashing out from the tire, threatening the gas tank.

They hit a parked car she and ricocheted into the street again, around the oncoming car. A bullet hole, like a spider web, appeared in the windshield. Marston was shooting at them, but he was almost a block behind now.

The Bentley was aflame and almost impossible to steer. They were coming fast downhill, toward an intersection, screeching and trailing smoke and fire.

Ahead of them the light turned red and a school bus started across the intersection. Nancy slammed her foot on the brake pedal. The Bentley swerved and skidded, and slowed hardly at all.

They were following trolley tracks that

turned sharply and disappeared into a tunnel. She put all the strength she had left into dragging the resisting wheel to the left.

The Bentley threw itself violently around. She thought it would turn over, and could do nothing more to control it.

19

Somehow, miraculously, they stayed upright and made it into the tunnel, bouncing and thumping over the rails. For an insane moment she thought they could drive through the tunnel and escape into its covering darkness, but one wheel was burning and another came off from the impact.

The car bucked and shuddered as if a giant hand had suddenly reached down to seize and stop it. The wheel was literally ripped out of her hands, and she was thrown across the seat against her father. They crashed in a roar of crumpled metal and broken glass and an incredible silence dropped over them. Gradually, sounds intruded — a dripping noise, the whirring of a tire spinning — and most ominous of all, the crackling of flames.

Her father moaned. 'Nancy?' he asked hoarsely.

'I — I think I'm all right.' She was numb with fear and shock and exhaustion.

'We've got to get out of here. The car's on fire.'

The door was stuck. The acrid smoke helped rouse her to action. Coughing and gasping for air, she pushed against the door on her side. Between the two of them, they managed to get it lifted up. They had to crawl up to get out, the hot metal burning her hands and legs. She dropped to the ground, landing painfully on metal railings. In a moment her father scrambled down beside her.

She would have liked to lay there, to sink into his arms and give herself up to the blackness within her that wanted to blend with the blackness of the tunnel.

'The car,' he mumbled.

With his help she got to her feet. They stood weakly for a moment, swaying together, each helping to hold the other upright while they tried to get their breath back.

Twin beams of light raked over them and someone shouted, 'Stay back — police!'

'Thank God,' Nancy said.

They started to shuffle clumsily along the tracks toward the headlight beams.

Someone crossed the light, running toward them, and she realized it wasn't the police at all. It was Marston.

'It's him,' she gasped, and jerked her father around, almost flinging him to the ground. They began to run in the opposite direction.

The two sides of the tunnel were separated by a wire fence. The Bentley had plowed through this, all but demolishing it, and they were on the opposite side now, on the side where the trolleys emerging from the tunnel would be travelling.

They ran through the opening in the fence to the other side, scrambling around the Bentley. A light appeared, and at first Nancy thought a trolley was coming. Then she realized it was one of the tunnel's lights, set back in an alcove. Ahead were dim points of lights at other alcoves, perhaps fifty feet apart.

Her father dragged her into the alcove, and a second or two later the ground shook and the tunnel flared with a ghastly light as the Bentley's gas tank exploded. Some debris flew by the little niche in which they sheltered, and something burning landed at Nancy's feet.

After a moment the flames died a little, and the sound of falling metal subsided. Nancy lifted a dirt-streaked face to her father. 'Do you think he . . . ?'

The Bentley had been between them and Marston when it exploded. If he had been going past it, he must surely have been killed.

'I'll see. You stay here.'

'No,' she said, dredging up whatever slim resources of courage and strength she had left. 'I'll come too.'

The car was still burning dispiritedly, giving out an eerie glow that flickered along the damp walls of the tunnel. The air was thick with acrid smoke and billowing dust raised by the explosion. Far in the distance she could just make out the sound of a siren, and she realized with a sense of shock that they had been in the tunnel no more than two or three minutes. It seemed a lifetime since the Bentley had plowed into that dark opening and then crashed. But the police were only just now on their way, summoned by God only knew which of the people they had passed by.

At first it looked as if the explosion had done in Marston. They could see back along the tunnel, to the light at the end, and he was not running along after them.

Then, as if her questioning look had summoned up the demon, there he was, dragging himself up from where he had fallen on the ground. He stood unsteadily for a moment, shaking himself as a dog shakes off the water from a river crossing. He saw them, Nancy behind her father attempting to shield her.

Marston had lost the gun. He started toward them.

'Stay behind me,' her father said.

Marston had come only a short distance, though, when the scene was suddenly interrupted by a brilliant flash of light and a deep rumble as if all the gods of Olympus were expressing their disapproval. The very ground beneath them shook, so that for a second Nancy thought they were having an earthquake, and she had a fleeting vision of the three of them buried beneath the tons of rubble as this mountain collapsed over them.

'The trolley.' Her father grabbed her and shoved her back toward the alcove. The car was rushing toward them on their side of the tunnel, and there was no room between car and walls for a man to stand, except in the alcoves that held the lights. Marston, seeing the trolley fast approaching, ducked into another of the alcoves.

It was their one chance to escape. 'Come on,' Nancy cried, seizing her father's arm.

Only a few yards from them was the tear in the fence that separated the two sections of track. If they could reach the opening and get onto the other side, they would have a chance to escape while the passing car on this side held Marston to his lighted alcove. It was a chance, albeit a slim one; and her father, now that they were on the tracks in front of the oncoming trolley, could do nothing but pray and run with her.

The trolley had slowed at the sight of the still-burning car on the opposite track, and it was this no doubt that enabled them to make their wild dash successfully. The ground trembled fearfully beneath them, and Nancy's heart pounded in her breast. She reached out for the fencing, grabbing a handful of twisted wire, and in the next second she was through, falling to her knees on the track. Her father fell across her and a fraction of a second later, the trolley went by. They felt the sucking of the wind that seemed to try to drag them toward the clacking wheels.

'We — got — to — run,' her father managed to gasp.

She tried to. She got to her feet with his help. They must have made, she thought, a pathetically silly looking pair of runners, clinging weakly to one another, neither of them barely able to lift one foot and put it before the other.

She couldn't think how much of a lead her ploy had given them over Marston; not enough, surely. Almost anyone could run faster than the two of them were moving, although she was straining every muscle in her body, exerting herself beyond every limit to try to find more strength.

The trolley had gone by now, a few startled or bewildered faces peering out from the lighted windows, trying to make out what on earth was going on out there in the darkness.

What was going on was that Nancy was finished; through. One foot slipped on a track and she tried to hold on to her father, but it was no good and she went down — not just to her knees, but flat on her face.

Her father half-knelt, half-fell beside her, tugging at her shoulders. 'Up,' he moaned.

She shook her head and said, 'Can't . . . just can't.'

And she was sure she couldn't, not if Marston himself pounced upon them the next second.

It wasn't Marston pouncing that got her to her feet again. Her father said, 'Trolley . . . another one.'

'Yes,' she gasped, not comprehending. 'Other side.'

Their conversation was not so much conversation as murmurs of breath that contained broken syllables of words. But she understood him with utter clarity when he mumbled in her ear, 'No, this side.'

She felt the earth beneath them beginning to tremble again, and with her face on the tracks like this, she could actually hear the rumble of the approaching trolley. The last car had passed on the other side, going into the tunnel. Now the trolley going in the opposite direction was shooting along the tunnel on their side of the fence.

She got to her knees, frantically sucking air into her lungs. In the distance they could see the dim pools of light from the alcoves. The nearest one on this side was at least thirty-five yards along — it looked like a thousand miles.

Somehow they got her to her feet, and turned back the way they had come — there was an alcove there not more than fifteen yards behind.

And not more than seven or eight yards beyond that was Marston, scrambling through the hole in the fence, looking altogether revived, and crazed with anger and frustration. There wasn't the slightest doubt he would kill them. Somewhere back along that side of the tunnel people were yelling and flashing lights. The police, no doubt.

Only, she and her father could not just stand here swaying to and fro with exhaustion, waiting for them to arrive. Long before the police got to this point, Marston would have reached them — or the trolley, coming from the opposite direction. On one side was a high, heavy wire fence — like clearing the Matterhorn in one jump — and on the other side, a solid wall.

Her father had assessed the situation a second or two faster than she, and yanked her violently around. 'Got to make it there,' he said, starting to run.

She knew he meant the lighted alcove along the track, but she was sure he was mad. She couldn't believe they could reach it. Even without a trolley coming, if she had been able to husband her strength and crawl in that direction, she wasn't sure she could have made it, let alone trying in pathetic desperation to run, scramble, jump — anything to propel them along, hands scraping the rough cement wall, tearing the flesh. The fire that had burned the Bentley was nothing to the fire blazing in her left side. She almost thought it would be easier to die than to go on like this, foot after foot, inch after inch, racing toward that distant pool of light that seemed almost to recede as they ran.

She had underestimated, though, the tenacity of the human life force, or the impact of total terror. The rumble and the shivering of the earth grew rapidly more pronounced, and in the distance they saw the trolley's headlight, like a giant yellow eye.

She ran as she had never run before, and in her fear-crazed mind she thought she might already have died, because it felt as if her feet weren't even touching those tracks. And still that pool of light seemed far, far away.

The train's eye grew until it wasn't an eye, but a glowing mouth that would swallow them up. The whole tunnel roared and shook as the infernal machine rushed toward them, closer, louder and brighter. The alcove was still ten yards away, the trolley no more than twenty or thirty yards behind that. The walls about them sweated with fear. The trolley shrieked a warning. Someone had seen them — too late to stop, too late, too late . . .

Five yards — three — two — and she was falling, her legs giving out, pitching forward, knowing that she was falling out of life, plunging into death; she had a vague impression of her father's hands dragging at her, pulling, and something seized the flare of her skirt and ripped it away from her legs, and behind her a man screamed, screamed as she had never heard a man scream before, and hoped never to hear again.

20

She could never say afterward by what miracle they had managed to reach that alcove with no more than a fraction of a second to spare. Her father had enough strength left, or had found enough, to grab at her as she stumbled, and his tug and the momentum of their flight had carried her to safety. But the escape had been narrow enough that the car in passing had caught the cloth of her skirt and torn most of it off.

The guardian angel that had saved them had closed his eyes, apparently, to Marston. He had started out in pursuit of Nancy and her father, too blind with rage to even notice that another trolley was coming. By the time he had realized the truth, he was halfway between two of the sheltering niches — too far away, and with too little time, to reach either of them. He had, perhaps carried along by his own momentum, tried for the same one that Nancy and her father had been able to reach. He was stronger, and almost managed to make up the extra distance — but not quite. The trolley, its conductor frantically trying to bring it to a stop, had caught him no more than ten feet — perhaps three yards — from the alcove, but the impact had sent him flying back several yards.

Of course, Nancy did not comprehend all this at once, or even realize the source of that soul-rending shriek she heard. For now, she could only lay huddled in her father's arms, gasping for breath, shivering with fear and exhaustion. She was dimly aware that they had escaped death, half-conscious that the trolley was now stopped inches away from her. She shuddered a little when it began to move again, slowly backing up, but she could no more have moved or stood or even screamed than she could have flown to the moon. If Marston had still been alive and in pursuit, he could have strangled her then and she would have made no effort to prevent him.

It was not Marston, though, who took hold of her, those strong hands upon her, pulling her gently from her father's embrace. She saw a policeman helping her father up, and knew that another was lifting her easily in strong arms, and she surrendered to the blackness at last, and sank gratefully into oblivion.

★ ★ ★

Aunt Polly's living room seemed filled with people. Detective Davis was there and Doctor Williams was in and out of the room, treating the cuts on Nancy's hands, and then rushing up to Aunt Polly's room. Nancy's father was there, as was Mick.

And of course there was Tom, sitting with a protective arm about Nancy's shoulders. She sank gratefully into the warmth of his embrace.

Detective Davis left the room, and came back after a few minutes to say that Mrs. Dunbar wanted to see Mr. Blair. Nancy's father went upstairs with him.

When he came down a short time later, it was evident that he had been crying. He came to the sofa where Nancy was sitting. 'She's suffering deeply for what she did,' he said. 'She begged me to forgive her, and asked me to look after you in the future.'

Nancy shook her head sadly. 'It's still so difficult for me to believe that Aunt Polly was behind all this tragedy and terror.'

'She didn't mean for it to get so out of hand. All she really wanted when she hired Marston were the jade figurines. She knew she had only a short time to live and she wanted to possess the entire set before she died. So she hired him to steal them, including her own to divert suspicion. But things got a little complicated.'

'Do you think she meant from the first to frame you for the robbery?'

Her father shrugged. 'I doubt it. I think I just seemed convenient. Things like this have a way of getting out of hand. One thing leads to another — it always seems obvious and inescapable — and the first thing you know, you're in over your head.'

Nancy turned to Tom. 'She must have suspected you were some sort of investigator when I described to her how you'd been following me around.'

'Probably,' Tom said. 'I think your father's right, though, that the woman simply never saw what she was doing in any sort of perspective. Like going for your father that day he was to meet you for lunch. Marston actually arranged the pickup, the same way he picked you up, by telling your dad you had been hurt and had sent for him. But I don't think your aunt thought ahead to what would have to be done once they had kidnapped him. Certainly she didn't want him to harm you, and she had never anticipated that he would murder Mrs. Leach.'

'What do you think will happen to her?' Nancy asked. 'Will she be charged and — '

'I wouldn't worry too much about that,' Tom told her. 'She has the money to hire a top lawyer, and given the fragile nature of her health, I don't think — '

'I want to go up to her,' Nancy interrupted. 'I can't condone the things she did, but I want her to know that I still care for her.'

'That's the strange thing,' her father said. 'I don't think Polly Dunbar ever really cared for anyone before; that's what surprised me when I talked to her just now. She loves you very much, Nancy.'

Nancy nodded thoughtfully as she got

to her feet. 'Yes. It's strange; I've spent all my life insisting no one loved me, when all the while everyone connected with me was trying to prove otherwise, and I didn't see it. I wasn't loving anybody. I was searching everywhere but inside myself. And of course, that's where you have to find it first.'

'The final irony,' Davis said, 'is that all this was done for the sake of those figurines; and after the fire and the explosion in the car, there's nothing left but some green dust and a few jagged pieces of jade.'

'And one statuette in Seattle,' Tom corrected.

'It's strange,' she said, looking from one to the other. 'Aunt Polly collected all of them but that one. And that one is the one representing happiness.'

She left them in a little group, and went up the stairs to see her aunt.

THE END

We do hope that you have enjoyed reading this large print book.

Did you know that all of our titles are available for purchase?

We publish a wide range of high quality large print books including:
Romances, Mysteries, Classics
General Fiction
Non Fiction and Westerns

Special interest titles available in large print are:
The Little Oxford Dictionary
Music Book, Song Book
Hymn Book, Service Book

Also available from us courtesy of Oxford University Press:
Young Readers' Dictionary
(large print edition)
Young Readers' Thesaurus
(large print edition)

For further information or a free brochure, please contact us at:
Ulverscroft Large Print Books Ltd.,
The Green, Bradgate Road, Anstey,
Leicester, LE7 7FU, England.
Tel: (00 44) **0116 236 4325**
Fax: (00 44) **0116 234 0205**

THE DOCTOR'S DAUGHTER

Sally Quilford

Whilst the Great War rages in Europe, sleepy Midchester is pitched into a mystery when a man is found dead in an abandoned house. Twenty-four-year-old Peg Bradbourne is well on the way to becoming a spinster detective, but it is a role she is reluctant to accept. When her stepmother also dies in suspicious circumstances, Peg makes a promise to her younger sister, putting aside her own misgivings in order to find out the truth.

SERGEANT CRUSOE

Leslie Wilkie

Luke Sharp is unaware that he has a double — Marco Da Silva, the ruthless criminal gang leader known as 'Silver'. When a pair of vigilantes intent on taking their revenge against Silver shoot Luke by mistake, his life is changed dramatically. Convalescing at his grandfather's home, he agrees to transcribe the old man's wartime memoirs of his exploits in the South Pacific. However, Silver finds out about Luke, and attempts to coerce him into work as his double in crime . . .

HOUSE OF FOOLS

V. J. Banis

Toby Stewart has been invited by her sister Anne to visit her at Fool's End, the manor where she works as a personal secretary to a famous author, and after his recent death has stayed on to catalogue his papers and manuscripts. But on arriving, Toby is dismayed to learn that Anne has mysteriously disappeared — without taking any of her possessions and without informing her employers. And most everyone there, it seems, has something to hide. Did Anne leave of her own volition — or has she perhaps been murdered . . . ?

DEATH VISITS KEMPSHOTT HOUSE

Katherine Hutton

Nick Shaw, travel writer and enthusiastic archer, expects to spend an enjoyable weekend with his partner, Louisa, at the luxurious Kempshott House Hotel. Then a body is discovered during an archery club contest on the hotel's grounds, stuck through with three arrows. The police are called in, assisted by Louisa — a detective sergeant — and it soon becomes apparent that the man has been deliberately murdered. Worse still, it would appear that the murderer hasn't finished yet . . .